FROM THE OTHER SIDE

Maja Padgett

ATHENA PRESS
LONDON

FROM THE OTHER SIDE
Copyright © Maja Padgett 2004

All Rights Reserved

No part of this book may be reproduced in any form
by photocopying or by any electronic or mechanical means,
including information storage or retrieval systems,
without permission in writing from both the copyright
owner and the publisher of this book.

ISBN 1 84401 240 9

First Published 2004 by
ATHENA PRESS
Queen's House, 2 Holly Road
Twickenham TW1 4EG
United Kingdom

Printed for Athena Press

FROM THE OTHER SIDE

Contents

Hamburg, 1950	9
Before Marta's Time	14
A Chosen Libra	15
A Penny for Keeps	17
A Guardian Angel – 1925	19
Old Tradition Comes to Mind	21
A New Year	24
Fashing Time	25
The Final Break	27
Passing Entertainment	29
The Mood of Play	31
A Fearful Visit	34
Pleasant Memories	35
A New Attraction	36
Family Entertainment	38
School Days	40
A Merry-go-round	42
A Lodger	44
A Passing	47
A Serious Occasion	48
Boy Meets Girl	50

A New Power	53
Camp Life	55
A Night March	58
The Mascot	60
A Cat's Dilemma	62
The Happy Wanderers	64
Land Army	66
Marien Hof	68
Rural Freedom	70
Riding for Pleasure	72
Working the Season	74
Marta's Downfall	76
Threshing Day	79
Potato Picking	81
Farewell Marien Hof	83
Meet the Other Half	85
Oh, My Papa	87
A Blanket on the Ground	91
Return to Hamburg	96
Moral Conflicts	98
Teenagers' Pleasures	101
A Birthday Drama	102
A Party Invitation	105
Turning Point	108
A Foolish Hero	109

Fire Duties	112
The Red Omen	114
To Be or Not to Be	119
Uncle Heini is Found Safe	121
Surrender	125
Aftermath: Humiliation	126
A Canoe called Peterle	129
Another Reunion	131
Unsafe Condition	133
A Lucky Meeting	137
Adaptation Essential	139
Teddy	141
Friendly Persuasion	142
Shared Pleasure	145
A Band of Gold	147
Arriving at Harwich	148
Tone Vale	152
A Birthday Present	156
Blackpool	157
Wedding Bells	159

Hamburg, 1950

MARTA SAT IN THE LABOUR EXCHANGE WAITING ROOM, A dejected figure recently made redundant. For the past two years she had been working at the British Military Hospital in the officers' quarters. She had enjoyed the work and had learned the English language with the help of the officers.

Bored with waiting, Marta looked at the display of posters on the walls. One caught her eye; it was asking for volunteers to work in Great Britain. She walked over to read the small print; it was the last week for acceptance… At that moment her name was called.

There was a job for her, as an office cleaner. Thoughts were racing through her head, *Once a cleaner, always a cleaner. There is no chance to rise above this. Such is the present system in Germany…* Her mother's face appeared before her eyes, worn out and old before her time through years of cleaning schools. The decision had to be taken now. Marta took a deep breath.

'About volunteers for work in Great Britain…' she asked the assistant.

She was sent to another department where she was kept waiting once more. She began to feel uneasy and nervous and was tempted to walk away. At that moment a lady came and asked if she could help her. When Marta explained that she was interested in working in Great Britain, the lady enquired where she had worked previously, and had she any references? When Marta showed her the reference from the officers, the lady was impressed.

'Do you speak English?' she asked.

'Yes,' Marta proudly replied.

The lady smiled and immediately filled in a form stating Marta's credentials. Marta was then informed that she would be hearing from them in due course…

Thinking deeply about the interview, Marta made her way

home from the city. Arriving hungry and tired at the flat where she rented a room she was met by her landlady, who handed her a letter. It was from England...

Quickly Marta stepped into her room and with trembling hands opened the letter. Stuart had kept his promise to write, and with every word he reassured her of his love. Tears flowed down her cheeks on to the pages.

After drinking a cup of coffee and having something to eat, Marta read the letter over and over again. Looking at a photograph of Stuart embracing a happy Marta, she daydreamed of the times they had been together. Horse riding in the country away from the busy city had been one of their favourite pastimes. Marta did not notice darkness falling as she recalled their embraces, his gentle way of touching her hair and calling her beautiful... She remembered the look on his face when he'd said how proud he would be to marry her – could this dream come true? Many British soldiers had promised marriage to other German girls, and Marta was well aware of the fact that once back home in England it all faded and they were shunned by their own people, outcast because they had fraternised with the ex-enemy so soon after hostilities...

Marriage was a very serious business as far as Marta was concerned. This belief was born out of her childhood without her father and the manner in which her parents' divorce had split the whole family. She remembered her mother working all day and ageing very early. She wanted to make sure her own marriage would last.

Marta eagerly awaited news from the Labour Exchange. Meanwhile Stuart's letters highlighted every day, giving her the strength and support needed. She dared not mention her having volunteered for work in Great Britain in case it did not work out, so as not to disappoint him.

Then one morning a letter *did* arrive from the Labour Exchange – she was instructed to go there on a certain date and to take her identity card, medical card and character references.

Anxiously Marta travelled once more into the city of Hamburg to the Labour Exchange. She was shown to a room where other girls sat waiting. Then it was her turn to be interviewed. She was asked many questions: family history; medical history; had she been in trouble with the law? All the information she gave them was checked thoroughly. She was then given a date and place for a medical. Out of many girls who applied to work in Great Britain only ten passed their medical. Happily, Marta was one of them. On 23 May 1950 Marta received a card stating she was:

'...accepted as suitable for employment in Great Britain.'

As soon as she knew the date she was to travel on, Marta began to dispose of the few possessions she had. The radio went to Kate and her furniture to her landlady. All she kept were some photographs, clothes and of course the Waldzitta which had belonged to Hans. For something to wear during the crossing Marta transformed her brother's special uniform which was left at home for use when he was on leave. She removed the military braid, rank-marking and buttons and then covered the buttons with black velvet. The trousers she made into a skirt, and the whole outfit was then dyed black. Satisfied with the result, Marta was ready '...*have date, will travel...*'

The date for departure was 17 July 1950. All the girls were instructed to assemble at the Altona railway station. Marta could not sleep the night before, and she was pale and nervous as she prepared to leave the flat. She looked out for Mutti, who should have been there, but there was no sign of here. This added to Marta's distress and rising tension. 'Oh, Mutti! How could you?' she cried. There was no turning back now – she had made her decision and was determined to see it through.

Picking up her few belongings, she said goodbye to her landlady and walked to the nearest Bahn station, still looking out for Mutti. Feeling rather disturbed, Marta boarded the train for Altona, not as happy as she had expected to be. She watched all the familiar places and stations with their memories flashing by. She alighted at Altona, her attention absorbed in finding the platform for the final departure from her homeland.

Some girls were already there, with their mums and dads. A lady from the Labour Exchange gave them their last instructions and then handed the papers over to Marta... she was put in charge of this consignment – she was senior in years to the others and had knowledge of English; this made her the natural choice. Marta felt that the importance of her status was a good omen for the new life she was beginning. But this did not lessen the sadness she felt because no one had come to see her go. No one cared – where was Mutti? Marta scanned the crowd in hope of seeing that loving face... there were only mums and dads in tears as their daughters boarded the train.

Disappointed, Marta stepped inside the train, trying to hide her emotion. *Be brave, little heart*, she murmured to herself, as she wiped the tears from her eyes. Suddenly, she thought she saw a familiar face, and before she knew it she was pacing the window, running along the corridor to see if it was an illusion. She gazed out of another window and there, on the platform, stood Uncle Heini and Aunty Julia, the two people Marta respected most. Their presence showed the affection they found so hard to express.

It was a touching last goodbye, with Julia promising to let Marta know Mutti's reason for not being there. Marta promised to write as soon as a residence in England was arranged. They wished Marta good luck as the train slowly left the station. She waved a white handkerchief until they were out of sight.

The train picked up speed, leaving Hamburg behind. Marta settled in with some of the girls, finding out their reasons for seeking work in England. Surprisingly, not many of them even understood English. What difficulties they were going to face!

Marta's thoughts turned to Stuart; what would he say when he knew that she had arrived in England...?

After a long train ride to the hook of Holland and through customs, Marta finally stood on the deck of the boat waiting to cross the English channel, she watched the activities below as the crew prepared for the departure.

Slowly the boat moved away from the quayside and headed for the open sea. As the coastline disappeared through the twilight, tears filled Marta's eyes and a wave of anxiety swept over her. Was she going in the right direction, she asked herself. England was unknown to her, in every aspect. She was a German subject. How would the English people react to this?

The impact of what she had done suddenly hit her. This was not a dream; this was for real. If she had not seen the poster in the Labour Exchange she would still be in Hamburg now among familiar places and faces…

As she watched the boat cleaving through the calm sea and felt the fresh salt air cooling her face, Marta felt a great sadness at leaving her homeland. If she had not fallen in love with Stuart she doubted very much that she would have taken such a step. Then she thought of her brother, Heinrich, coming home from a prisoner-of-war camp to find his home gone and destruction everywhere in Leipzig where he'd lived. A disappointed man, he had made his decision to start a new life. He chose Canada as his new country.

Now it was Marta's turn. Maybe Lady Luck was on her side for a change. She went down to her cabin, and as she lay on her bunk bed listening to the hum of the engine her mind lapsed into the turbulent past she was leaving behind.

Before Marta's Time

WORLD WAR ONE WAS ON THE HORIZON WHEN MARTA'S mother and father got married. Their first-born was a beautiful looking girl; they called her Klara. Shortly after war broke out her father had to leave to fight for his fatherland. Her mother was pregnant again, and during her father's absence, a boy was born. He was named Hans by his mother, and for three years she struggled to look after the children on her own.

The war was over and their father returned to family life. Fortunately he came through the hostilities unscathed and soon found a job as a print setter, being a skilled man in this trade.

Very soon her mother was pregnant again. This time she had twin boys. One died four hours after birth. The other baby was delicate but survived and was called Heinrich.

Now, all should have been well – three lovely children: Klara, with her golden hair and fine, classic looks; Hans with red hair and a turned-up nose; and Heinrich whose beauty equalled that of his sister, with golden ringlets and fine features.

Even by the low financial standards of the 1920s the family lived in a very comfortable flat in a cul-de-sac: it consisted of three fairly big rooms divided by a small passage. There was also a kitchen and pantry and at the end of the passage was a toilet. It was a luxury in those days to have an indoor flush toilet. Every room had gas light and two rooms had a small stove in the corner for heating.

A stairway, which led to six other apartments, also gave access to a large attic where each tenant had a designated place to store coal and wood, or whatever.

A Chosen Libra

WITH THREE YOUNG CHILDREN AND PREGNANT ONCE more following a miscarriage, Mother could not cope, and quarrels became more and more frequent, mostly about the untidiness, which Father found disgusting. Marta's untimely arrival did little to help the unhappy situation.

At seven months pregnant her mother was rushed into hospital and gave birth to a baby girl, weighing only two and a half pounds. She was immediately put into an incubator, but the doctor held little hope for her survival.

When her father arrived at the hospital later, not seeing a baby near her mother he presumed it to be dead.

His words – 'just as well, one mouth less to feed' – horrified her mother. She remembered those hurtful words for the rest of her life, and often spoke of them in later years.

However, the tiny scrap of humanity in the incubator surprised everyone by thriving on her mother's milk. She was already showing the survival instinct which was to stand her in good stead always. Her mother named her Marta and the love she had for her tiny baby was strong. There was a special bond between them throughout their lives.

The new addition meant another mouth to feed, and that did not help the situation at home. It led to the break-up of the already floundering marriage. Her father left and went to Leipzig, his birthplace. His parents lived there, owning a coal merchant's business. He took Klara, his beautiful daughter, with him.

He left Mother to care and provide for the other three children. In those days there was no law of protection for the wife as there is today. What a terrible situation to be in. This was only the beginning of years of hardship for poor Mother…

Hans, the older brother, tried to help by tidying the flat after school and taking on a paper round for very little money. He just wanted to make life easier for his mother.

15

Time passed and the Easter arrived when Marta was to start school. Mother had to find a little satchel, which was strapped on to her back and a special treat was a cornet-shaped container with fancy trimmings on the outside filled with lovely sweets of all shapes and sizes. Marta was so proud and excited as she went off with Mother to be enrolled as a pupil.

At the school she was so busy watching the other girls and scrutinising their cornets that she did not notice Mother had left her.

After school, Heinrich, who attended the boys' part of the school, was going to take her home each day. He was a big boy against Marta's little shape, and it made her feel protected. Mother would be out cleaning schoolrooms at that time, and this meant leaving Heinrich and little Marta without supervision after coming home from school.

Mostly Heinrich went to a coal merchant's yard to help out with the horses, but Marta was too young to join him and had to play with other little children in the cul-de-sac where they lived.

A Penny for Keeps

ONE DAY MOTHER LEFT A NOTE FOR HEINRICH, ASKING him to do some shopping for her. The money was on top of it. Marta decided to go with him just to have a good look at all the fascinating jars of sweets on the shelves.

After Heinrich had bought the bread and margarine he took her hand and led her outside. There was a penny change from the shopping and Marta noticed this.

'We can have some sweets with that,' she said, looking at Heinrich's face to see what his reaction would be.

'Of course we can't! What if Mother finds out?'

'She may not,' Marta said, and she waited as temptation overruled her brother's common sense.

'All right then, just this once,' he said, as he led her back into the shop.

The shrilling of the doorbell made them both jump, although it hadn't bothered them the previous time.

'What do you want?' the shopkeeper asked, peering at them over the counter. Heinrich gave him the penny and they chose the sweets they wanted. It was sheer magic to them. They hurried home, savouring a bon-bon in their mouths and still happily chewing.

Their pleasure was short-lived. Mother had arrived home earlier than usual. As Heinrich handed her the bread and margarine she noticed that both her children were chewing; she could smell sweets.

'Open your mouths this instant!' she commanded. 'Where did you get the money for those from?'

Shamefacedly Heinrich told her. Mother was so angry, but hadn't the heart to punish them. Instead she told them to go across to their grandmother, who lived nearby. She also instructed them to tell her the whole story. They knew what that meant. Grandmother was strict and feared more than loved by the children. They walked slowly and finally stood there facing the door, pushing each other to do the knocking. Heinrich fell against the door and the door flew open. Grandmother must have heard the commotion.

'What is the matter?' she asked Heinrich, her face stern and uncompromising. She took them into the kitchen and there Heinrich stammered out the story. Without warning she hit him hard then turned to Marta, who defiantly clutched a sticky sweet in her hand as she took her punishment, shedding a tear...

A Guardian Angel – 1925

During the winter of that year snow covered the ground, and children of all ages enjoyed snowballing and racing on their sleighs. In the midst of all the activity were Marta and Heinrich, snatching a ride here and there. The news was spreading that a big pond, about half an hour's walk away, was frozen and children were skating on it. Marta wanted to go, but Heinrich did not really want to walk so far. 'Please take me,' his little sister pleaded.

'Oh, all right, Marta, but only for a short time.'

Heinrich could usually be persuaded by the determined little girl, often against his better judgment (as in the case with the sweets).

When they arrived at the pond there was already a big crowd present. They joined a long queue of youngsters who were just sliding across the ice. Marta's little legs kept giving way on the slippery surface, and fast-moving skaters kept shouting at her to get out of the way. In the mêlée she became parted from Heinrich and began to panic because she could not keep her balance long enough to move away from the area.

Suddenly, the weight of too many people caused the ice to begin to crack, and it gave way just where Marta was standing, taking her down into the black, icy water. The crowd, silent now, looked in horror at the gaping hole with the little figure frantically trying to get hold of the edge, which broke off as soon as she touched it.

No one dared help her: they all backed away from the danger of the breaking ice. Heinrich, who had been searching for his little sister among the crowd, realised it was Marta desperately fighting for her life. With no thought of the danger, he tried to pull her out, but in doing so fell in himself. Still no one attempted to help them, but a guardian angel must have taken pity, giving Heinrich enough strength to pull himself out onto the ice, which miraculously did not give way. Lying flat on his stomach he managed to drag an exhausted Marta out of the water too.

Unfortunately, their ordeal was not yet over; they had a long way to walk home and their clothes froze to their bodies. It was getting dark and they knew Mother would be home now, getting worried. Oh, she would be angry with them when she knew what had happened!

Teeth chattering and in agony from the freezing cold cloth on their bodies, they eventually arrived home. Mother was so angry when she saw the state of their clothes that without asking why she smacked them both and sent them to bed, but not into a cosy warm bed like most people enjoy in these modern times. Within a short time both Heinrich and Marta were running high fevers and were delirious.

It was Hans who first noticed when he went in to see them. He fetched Mother and they quickly heated bricks in the oven, wrapped them in newspaper and put them by the children. It was too late; obviously both children were seriously ill and Mother had to call in the doctor.

His diagnosis was pneumonia and both were in a critical condition. Hans was sent to the *apotheke* (chemist) with the doctor's prescription, while Mother was told to put cold compresses on their foreheads to get the fever down.

This was 1925, and these sorts of illnesses had to be dealt with at home. Neither were there any antibiotics in those days. Miraculously the children did survive. Heinrich recovered long before Marta – he had much more strength. Mother was very distressed to see Marta so ill. By now she had been told about the incident that had led to all this, and she regretted her harshness to the children when they had arrived home. She tried to bring strength to her little girl by bringing her whatever treats she could afford. Marta was very weak for a long time and temporarily blinded. Mother even borrowed some money from Grandma so that she could buy a little doll. She took it home and said to Marta, 'There is a new doll standing at the bottom of your bed.' This was to encourage her to fight back, to want to see that doll. Her strategy worked; Marta responded by struggling to open her swollen, matted eyes. It was a slow progress, but once more she fought her way back from the brink. The family rejoiced as she slowly regained her health and strength. What a tough little character she was underneath that frail exterior!

Old Tradition Comes to Mind

ONCE MORE IT WAS DECEMBER AND CHRISTMAS WAS approaching. Marta was making her way home from school. She walked past the shops and was enchanted by the Christmas decorations and toys in some of the windows. The centre of attraction she was concerned with was a rocking horse, grey with brown spots and a long, flowing mane and tail. Her nose pressed flat against the window, she was dreaming and she was wishing it could be hers...

In her fantasies she was on its back and the feeling was wonderful. Coming out of her dreams she realised that it was getting dark and started running for home. No one was there when she arrived; Heinrich had to stay on at school, Hans was doing his paper round and Mother was working at her cleaning job.

Resignedly, Marta sat on the cold, dark stairs awaiting Mutti's return. She daydreamed about the rocking horse while she sat there, knowing that it was an impossible dream.

At school preparations for Christmas were starting. They were taught how to make an *Adventkranz*. Fir tree branches were firmly fixed to a circle of strong wire in the fashion of a wreath. Long silk ribbons were then fastened at equal points and brought together to a hanging position. A large decorative bow was then added. Four candles in holders were then placed between the ribbons. The *Adventkranz* was then completed and ready to hang up. On the first Advent Sunday one candle would be lit, and one more each following Sunday until Christmas arrived.

How Marta loved the special atmosphere of Christmas Eve! To her young mind it held a secrecy which seemed to spread over the whole world; a hush of expectancy, as children were on their best behaviour, wondering what kind of presents they would receive.

Mother was walking around with a glow in her eyes, and this

in itself pleased the children because her eyes were usually dull. She gave her children strict instructions not to go into her bedroom.

The Christmas tree was not seen until Christmas Eve. While the children played outside Mutti smuggled the tree into the flat. It was a real one, of course; no imitation ones in those days. Mutti hung chocolate rings and decorations on the tree, then fixed tiny candles in holders to the tree to complete the ritual. The small oven in the kitchen was working overtime, as pails of water were heated to tip into a small bath which was placed close to the oven so that the water did not have to be carried far. Each of the children were fetched and after their bath were dressed in their best clothes.

Mutti had prepared a special meal for them all. After they had eaten she went into the other room while the children waited expectantly until they heard a little bell ringing. Very quietly, not running, they stepped into the Christmas room, seeing the Christmas tree for the first time.

The spell of that moment cannot be described to children of today. Its magic warmed the little home. They were so humble in their upbringing they enjoyed the peaceful atmosphere.

Even at that early age Marta felt a peace which she never forgot. Always at Christmas she would reflect and recall the simplicity and spirit of the Christmas Eves of her childhood…

The two younger children recited Christmas poetry they had learned at school, while Hans and Mutti listened and duly applauded at the end. Then altogether they sang 'O Tannenbaum' and the little tree seemed glorified, standing there in glistening beauty and light. The glow of the candles was reflected in their eyes as they gazed at it.

Now it was time for present giving, and Marta gasped as Mutti pulled something out from behind the Christmas tree. It was a rocking horse! In Marta's eyes it was just like the one in the shop window, but in reality it was one that Mutti had been fortunate to buy second-hand.

'Oh, Mutti,' Marta cried. 'How did Father Christmas know? Could he hear all the wishing and praying when I was looking into the shop window?'

Mutti looked at the excited little girl, not quite sure what to say, as Marta jumped onto the rocking horse, which had been bought for Heinrich, of course. There was a big doll for Marta, but she hadn't even glanced at it. Mutti looked at her daughter's excited face as she rocked to and fro, shouting commands to the horse as if it were alive. She was squealing with sheer delight...

While Heinrich stood looking calmly at the doll trying to understand Marta's choice, Hans watched this scene with amusement, but neither he nor Heinrich said anything to spoil Marta's obvious joy. Observing her children's reactions, Mother thought how very different to one another they were. After giving Hans his present, Mutti signalled for the boys to follow her out of the room. Marta didn't even notice when they left her for a few minutes. The three of them agreed not to spoil Marta's fun by telling her that she had made a mistake. They would explain the situation next morning. Heinrich said, 'Marta can share the rocking horse with me in any case.'

Mutti felt proud of her son's unselfishness, and vowed to try and buy him some little treat after Christmas to show him much she appreciated his decision.

As the holy night ended, Marta and Heinrich went to bed. Tired from all the excitement they were soon asleep, happily dreaming into Christmas Day...

Mutti and Hans looked at them as they went to their own beds. Seeing them so rosy-cheeked, clean and well fed, Mutti thought how lovely it was to see them so contented. She wished that every day could be like this...

A New Year

NEW YEAR'S EVE WAS QUITE THE OPPOSITE TO CHRISTMAS Eve; the atmosphere was noisy and gay. A large bowl of punch was prepared during the day, mixing various wines and spirits, fruit juices etc.: the stranger the taste, the better. No one really measured quantities; it seemed part of the fun, finding out the final result of this (often very potent) mixture...

The whole flat smelled of baking. Cakes, doughnuts and biscuits would be served from ten o'clock onwards. The children had fireworks and delighted in scaring people they disliked by placing jumping frogs through their letter box. Half the fun was running away to escape being caught and punished.

By the time midnight arrived the whole street was a scene of gaiety and excitement. On the stroke of midnight fireworks exploded in the sky and the whole place seemed to go mad. There was the noise of exploding fireworks and people shouting 'Happy New Year!' to each other, shaking hands (without the kissing). A hot doughnut was eaten with relish, as the cold air immediately froze the breath.

Gradually the crowd dispersed into dance halls. Men gathered in their local pubs and house parties were very popular, judging by the sound coming from the closed windows. The street was once more empty except for a drunk swaying as he wound his way home.

The darkness was relieved by a few gas lamps and the lights shining from windows where parties were in full swing, celebrating a new year – good or bad, and the moment was enjoyed till dawn.

Fashing Time

AFTER THE NEW YEAR FESTIVITIES CAME 'FASHING TIME'. THIS was a novel annual event when there were fancy-dress dances and great fun was had by all as friends bet among themselves that they would recognise whoever was to be their quarry before midnight. Everyone wore a mask, so this would prove quite difficult. Many were the surprises when the revellers unmasked the wrong partners as the clock struck twelve.

This was one time when Mutti had fun; she loved dancing – this Marta had inherited. The rest of the year was hard work and worry with no husband to love and care for her.

On this happy occasion it lifted her spirits, and for that short time she enjoyed herself in choosing a stylish costume that would have been beyond Mutti's means if she had not been lucky enough to have a friend who was a dressmaker. Out of pieces of material her friend gave to her they spent many hours planning and making their costumes.

Marta was too young to understand many things, but she always remembered the happy mood Mutti was in at that time. She loved seeing her mother happy.

Mutti's friend had a son, a little older than Marta, and the children played happily together while their mothers were busy. The boy had lots of toy animals, which Marta loved playing with, but he preferred reading, so she let him have her treasured book *Lederstrumpf* (*The Last of the Mohicans*) while she enjoyed herself with the animals.

On the night of the ball Mutti was getting dressed when her friend arrived with her son, who was going to stay the night with Hans and Marta. They were given some sweets and promised to be good. Mutti came out of the bedroom and paraded in front of the children.

'Oh, Mutti,' Marta cried, 'you look like a princess!'

Her costume was stunning, representing a chessboard cleverly designed from black and white satin. The bodice was black on one side and white on the other, while the pants showed off her well-shaped legs and were beautifully made. Her tall hat came to a point with a veil attached, and her face was covered by a black satin mask with a lace insert to cover her mouth.

She looked wonderful to Marta; a different person, glowing with anticipation of pleasures to come... she left with her friend in such a happy mood.

What a lucky night it was for her, too. She won a bet and also first prize for her costume.

The Final Break

THE FOLLOWING YEAR WAS NOT TO BE A GOOD ONE FOR Mutti. Marta vaguely remembers the day her father arrived unexpectedly at the flat...

Tall, handsome with bushy hair and penetrating grey eyes, he was a dominant figure. He went with Mutti into another room and the children heard raised voices as a heated argument took place. The door was flung open and her father called Heinrich and told him to get dressed for travelling. He paid little attention to Marta, who was bewildered by what was going on. Mutti came out of the room, white-faced and crying. She held Marta close to her as Father and Heinrich, a boy of seven, walked out of the flat.

Mutti's golden-haired son was going away for good. He was going to live with Father and sister Klara in Leipzig where he would receive a better education and more of the material things in life. In her innocence Marta did not understand the significance of this moment, she only knew that her beloved Mutti was crying and that her father, who had always shown her that she was of no importance to him, was taking Heinrich away from them.

She felt nothing for this man who had caused them unhappiness, but she felt Mutti's love for her as she held her tight. This strong bond between them never failed when they faced many trials in their future lives.

In later years Father was to pay for his folly. He never thought that children conceived in a moment of pleasure would one day grow up and with minds of their own know where their loyalty must be...

Life went on, but it was hard. Even with one mouth less to feed (the very words used by Father when he thought Marta had died at birth) it was difficult for Mutti to make ends meet.

Hans, seven years Marta's senior, was busy with his paper rounds and doing any odd job he could to earn money to help

Mother. Shortly after Heinrich had been taken away, Mutti and Father were finally divorced and the family was split for ever, the two golden-haired children stayed with their father. They were well-fed and clothed and received a very good education. The two red-haired children, who were left with their mother, were to know hardship for many years.

Marta spent more time on her own now that Heinrich wasn't around. She was given small tasks to do while Hans was on his paper round. One was to peel the potatoes and put them on to cook at a certain time. Of course she preferred to be playing outside with other children. With no one there to control her actions she was running wild, a real tomboy always willing to join in games with neighbouring children, mostly boys. They teased her about her red hair, calling her carrot face. When she was challenged to a race by bigger boys, she was always ready to get set and go! Her skinny little legs would invariably get her to the winning post first, indicating that even then she had the status of a ringleader.

She gave orders as to who were to be the cowboys or the indians. Sometimes she would pretend she was a white horse, the fastest in the world, of course. Other times she would be in a travelling circus, standing on a horse's head or doing flickflacks... The hours passed quickly in this imaginary world of childhood. Somebody mentioned the time: oh my goodness! Potatoes to peel and cook!

Marta raced upstairs to the flat, found a few potatoes and started to peel them. The peeling came away thicker than the potato left behind, but she managed to put them on the gas ring and light it. Now she dashed outside again to play for a little while longer; a disastrous decision. When she went back to the flat, thinking they would be nicely cooked, the acrid smell of burnt potatoes was everywhere, the place full of smoke. She quickly found a few more potatoes and put them in another saucepan to cook, hiding the burnt saucepan in the hope no one would notice what had happened...

What a hope! When Mutti arrived home the flat still reeked of burning. Marta was given a good hiding and was sent to bed hungry. The lesson was learned for a few days and then forgotten.

Passing Entertainment

OCCASIONALLY AN OLD TRAMP APPEARED IN THE CUL-DE-sac where Marta and her family lived. The children greeted him excitedly as soon as they recognised him. Under his arm he carried a sack and after he had picked a spot he took a little stool out of his sack and placed it on the ground. As soon as he sat down on it, the children gathered around him. He then produced a saw from his sack, which he put between his legs, and using a small bow he would produce a strange wailing sound, bending the saw to vary the pitch.

Windows started to open and people threw money down wrapped in paper, and the children took great pride in picking the money up, unwrapping it and putting it into the old man's cap, which he placed on the ground. He would bow his head in a gesture of thanks towards the generous giver. The sound was so sad to Marta's mind as he vibrated high and low with the bending saw. The children enjoyed his coming, but it was illegal so he did not come very often.

Instead came an organ grinder with a little monkey fastened by a chain to the top of the organ. It did tricks and was very cute. Marta watched the monkey's antics, which fascinated her. She loved the way it looked straight at the children with big brown eyes.

The music was of course livelier than that made by the old man's saw.

Again the children picked up the money thrown from the windows, dancing and laughing as they did so. The organ grinder would bow his head to thank them whilst playing '*Odonna Klara*', and many other popular tunes of that time.

Another passing entertainment was a travelling circus. Sitting on hard benches around the small ring, everyone would be torn between excitement and fear as the high wire and trapeze artists defied death, performing without safety nets, balancing high above the up-turned faces of their audience as they were silhouetted against the sky. The performing dogs and clowns were great fun to watch. The show was ended with a donkey, inviting people to have a ride, but nobody managed; the donkey would throw them into the dust to the laughter of the applauding crowd. The circus would stay for about a week and then move on…

The Mood of Play

ONE OF THE PLEASURES WHICH MARTA ENJOYED WAS TO GO to a large park fairly close to her home. Here children from all around gathered to play on the various amusements. The vast sandpit was where Marta always made for; she loved to feel the sand between her bare toes and to build things or to play on the big wooden tree trunks buried in the sand. Her vivid imagination was able to run riot here. Then one day disaster struck. She lost the house key in the sand (it was like trying to find a needle in a haystack).

Children of all ages helped her as she frantically moved heaps of sand about, tears flowing down her face in fear of the punishment awaiting her because she had lost the key. After searching for a long time she faced up to the fact that she would never find it now.

On her way home she toyed with the idea of running away, but were to? Mother was coming down the street looking for her. 'What are you crying for?' she asked the weeping child.

Between sobs, Marta told her about the loss of the key. Angrily her mother chided her for being so careless, but didn't smack her in the street; that would be done behind closed doors. Understandably her mother was tired after working hard for hours and then to come home and find herself locked out of the flat was the last straw...

She had to borrow a ladder and enter the flat through a back window, which had fortunately been left open. Mother was so furious after her ordeal she hit Marta with a stick. The little girl had never seen her mother in such a temper, and was so petrified that she ran out of the flat, down the stairs and out into the street. She would have kept on running, but the sight of a wagon with her beloved horses in harness stopped her in her tracks. Without hesitation she just crawled under their bellies to hide and sat by the shaft between them, peeping from underneath to see if Mother was coming after her.

At the sight of a child under two heavy horses, people started to gather round trying to coax her out, asking her name. The lady from the bread shop recognised her and sent someone to fetch her mother. Now it was *her* turn to be petrified. One move of those hooves could have trampled Marta to death, or at least severely injured her, but the child's trust in her friends was rewarded. They stood motionless as Mutti begged Marta to come out, promising there would be no more hidings. Instead she would have a special treat on pay day. That was enough to bring her carefully out from her hiding place.

The following Thursday Marta went to where Mutti was working after school. Mutti saw her coming and called her to a classroom she was due to clean. First of all the stools had to be lifted up onto the desks then the floor was ready for sweeping. To think that Mutti had to do this six days a week for very little pay! Marta realised that Mutti was in need of love and care as much as herself. Overworked, harassed and very vulnerable, it was no wonder she had no patience with childish pranks and carelessness.

After several hours of cleaning classrooms and long corridors all the utensils had to be put back in a cupboard for use another day. Happy to have finished for the day they wound their way home, calling at a shop to buy the promised special treat – a bag of shrimps, peeling and eating them as they walked along.

With a spare penny Marta was then sent to a little factory nearby for a bag of broken biscuits. These biscuits did not last long, nor did the money, and by Tuesday Marta was sent to a little grocer's shop to get something to eat 'on tick' – to be paid for the next Thursday. This caused her great embarrassment, and if people were in the shop she let them be served until there was no one to hear her asking. Grown-ups did not seem to realise the deep feelings of a sensitive child. Marta loved Mutti so she did what was asked of her without question, but the way she felt about it made such a deep impression on her that in years to come she vowed to do much better for herself in life than Mutti had done. It was a valuable lesson learned in those early days…

These past chapters have been about a child's life up to the early 1930s when horses were still used in busy cities. Children of that era were poor maybe, but they were respectful to other people: they greeted neighbours with courtesy; a boy would take off his cap and bow in greeting without being told to do so; running errands for the elderly was a pleasure and children felt important doing these things. If they were rewarded with a penny this was much appreciated. The social attitudes were strict; to call someone by their first name was only done within the family circle or close friends, otherwise it was Mr and Mrs – very formal…

A Fearful Visit

PARENTAL WARNINGS ABOUT VARIOUS THINGS HAD NEVER bothered Marta very much until the day she saw gypsies appear in the cul-de-sac where she was happily playing. The other children were panic stricken when they saw two gypsy women coming towards them. They ran to the safety of their homes and mothers for protection. For Marta there would be no Mother for comfort… running as fast as her little legs would carry her, with pounding heart she flew up the stairs and with shaking hands she tried to put the key into the lock. It seemed to take a lifetime to open the door, rush inside and close it again. Hurriedly she locked the door and put the safety chair on for extra security. Then she huddled into a corner, waiting and listening as footsteps slowly came nearer and nearer to the flat door…

They stopped and there was knocking on the door, Marta held her breath in fear of being heard outside. The gypsy knocked again – louder this time – sending shivers through the frightened little girl. Then there was silence. Presumably the gypsy was peeping through the keyhole. Slowly the footsteps moved across to the neighbour's door, but they were out.

The gypsy determinedly went up to the flats above, but the old man who lived there sent her grumbling on her way. It seemed ages to Marta before those haunting, deliberate footsteps made the descent downstairs and out of the building. The sheer terror of this experience lingered inside her for quite a time.

Eventually she plucked up the courage to peer from behind the net curtains and make sure the gypsies had departed from the cul-de-sac. No children ventured outside to play again that day.

The reason for their fear was that – as the story goes – gypsies take naughty children away with them and sell them to strangers. That was why they wore shawls around their shoulders; to hide children under.

This the children believed…

Pleasant Memories

ONE OF MARTA'S PLAYMATES WAS TRAUDI WHO LIVED IN A flat directly opposite. Her mother was forever peering from behind her net curtains and was aware of all the happenings that occurred in the cul-de-sac. Frau Walter observed the fact that Marta was often alone in the flat. Sometimes when Marta was sitting in the window on a rainy day she would beckon her to come across. It never took her long to hurry down the stairs and up to Traudi's flat, which was warm, tidy and well furnished.

Traudi had a lovely room, with fabulous toys – nothing but the best. She was an only child whose parents cared a great deal. Time spent there was happy, despite a few battles between the two girls over a toy, as Traudi was rather spoiled, but differences were soon forgotten, as is the way with young children.

The best times they had together, as far as Marta was concerned, were in the summertime school holidays. She would go with Traudi and her parents to their allotment outside Hamburg. They had a lovely little wooden house where they stayed. Traudi's father would be away during the week at his work while her mother cultivated the surrounding land. What a lovely time the children had together!

Traudi was four years younger than Marta. There were pet rabbits in hutches – beautiful creatures – and often a neighbour's dog was taken for a walk. They picked fruit and watched Traudi's mother bottling it or making jam. All the things Marta missed at home and the memories of these carefree summer holidays stayed with her for ever.

A New Attraction

BACK HOME TO SCHOOL DAYS AND AWAY FROM THE countryside, Marta's thoughts still turned to animals. Quite near to her home was a coal merchant's yard and they had great big horses to pull their coal wagons. Marta found them fascinating creatures, and she had no fear of them at all. Herr Hadler, who owned the coal business, noticed the little girl gazing wistfully through the gates at the horses.

'Where do you come from?' he asked her. Marta pointed across the road to the flats.

'Do you like horses?' Herr Hadler enquired. She nodded shyly.

'Would you like to sit on one?'

'Yes please!' was the eager reply.

He lifted her up onto the huge back and told her to hold on to the coarse mane of this gentle horse. To Marta that was heaven. Frau Hadler came out of the house and asked her man, 'Who is this little girl?'

He told her that Marta came from the flats.

'Doesn't her mother mind, such a little girl spending her time around the yard where the horses are?' Frau Hadler persisted.

'She seems lonely,' he replied. 'Her mother is working, cleaning schools, and her brother does paper rounds, so she is left on her own quite often…'

He looked at the small figure still perched on the horse with a happy face. Smiling he remarked to his wife, 'She is hardy for all that, she is so skinny and has no fear of the horses at all. It is remarkable for one so young.'

The next time Marta ventured into the yard again Herr Hadler sent her into the house to see his wife.

Entering the large kitchen, Marta saw a little girl playing on the floor. This was the cherished daughter of the coal merchant and his wife. After Frau Hadler had given Marta a cake and a glass of milk she asked her if she would play with the little girl. Trying to be polite Marta sat on the floor and looked at what had appeared to her to be a pretty living doll, with large brown eyes and curly brown hair. She was so dainty and beautifully dressed! Marta was lost for words and wished she was outside in the dirty yard with her friends, the horses.

As soon as Frau Hadler went from the kitchen into another room she seized her chance to escape, running out of the kitchen, through the yard and back to the flats. Not daring to go back for a while, she found an old smithy in a small back street and spent hours beside the open doors watching the horses being shod. The thick, smelly smoke stinging her eyes did not deter her at all, but she did miss sitting on the big horses at the coal merchant's yard though.

One day as she was coming home from school on an old bike which a neighbour had loaned to her, she saw a pair of horses coming from a side street. They were not pulling a wagon and a man was leading them. Marta recognised her beloved Prinz and Hercules and saw that it was Herr Hadler leading them.

Marta stopped and asked him if she could take the horses home. The yard was only around the corner, and to her delight he agreed and lifted her up onto Hercules' back while he wheeled the bike. What a strange sight it was, to see a pair of big horses with a scrap of a girl proudly sitting on one and guiding them home! Of course they could easily have walked home on their own, they were so close to their stables and such intelligent, placid creatures.

Marta was in seventh heaven and thanked Herr Hadler over and over again. He was intrigued by this child who shared his love of horses and wished his own daughter had the same adventurous spirit…

Family Entertainment

GRANDMA'S FLAT WAS NEAT AND TIDY – VERY DIFFERENT from her daughter's. She was disappointed in Mutti's inability to cope with her home and children, but realised that the years of stress and strain, she had suffered through the despicable behaviour of her husband, had sapped her strength.

Every Thursday evening the grandparents were visited by Marta's Uncle Heini and Aunty Julia. Mutti usually went as well, and occasionally she took Marta with her. How she enjoyed this privilege! Marta had a great admiration for her Uncle and Aunty. They were a very refined couple and lived outside Hamburg. Uncle Heini worked at the meteorological office, but his great hobby was painting. He was an acknowledged artist. Aunty Julia worked as a dental technician, so with two incomes they were comfortably off. They had no children of their own, but Uncle Heini loved to play with Marta and tease her.

After the grown-ups had finished their weekly game of cards, he always played 'Tick' with her to see who would be touched last as they said goodnight. As Marta ran after him with a happy smile to tick Uncle Heini last, he would press a coin into her little hand. As she squealed with delight her mother would tell her to behave and come along.

When they reached home Mutti would ask what was in her hand and take the coin from her to be used for something desperately needed. It was always like that. Marta's bliss was very short-lived, but she accepted the situation, even at that tender age. Uncle Heini must have guessed what happened too…

On a rare occasion Mutti and Marta were invited to visit them, so in their Sunday best they had to travel on the S Bahn to Ohlsdorf. Uncle Heini and Aunty Julia would be there to meet them and they would walk together to their flat in a rural setting.

The flat was warm with central heating, and everywhere was furnished with great taste and there were lots of books and paintings showing the artistic interests Uncle Heini possessed. The table was set for an evening meal, with porcelain and silver cutlery.

These visits made a deep and lasting impression on Marta, and in later years she was to strive to create such a home for herself.

Uncle Heini was tall and slim and had a handsome face with very clear grey eyes. His manner was calm as he spoke to Aunty Julia. They shared a great respect for each other.

One of the best portraits he ever painted was of Grandma. It hung on the wall of one of the rooms in Mutti's flat. Marta would often look at it with awe. It was so lifelike the eyes seemed to follow you wherever you moved to. She sat there, her face stern as usual, her hair drawn tightly back into a bun as was the fashion for older people. In a sitting position, she wore a long dark skirt and a dark bodice. Everything was so drab, and yet in it solemn way it was a masterpiece…

School Days

AS TIME PASSED MARTA ENJOYED MOVING UP AT SCHOOL. She was not a clever pupil – probably because she found it difficult to pay attention. Her reports said that she was restless and untidy, but also said she had an outstanding talent in art, but Mutti was indifferent to this.

The teachers were impressed with her detailed drawings of horses and she was chosen to draw a horse on the blackboards in other classrooms. While watching the horses in the coal merchant's yard she had observed with a keen eye their shape and everything about them.

The fact that she was good at sport was also mentioned in her reports. She certainly had enough exercise; before going to school each morning Marta went across to the baker's to collect a large basketful of breakfast buns to take to customers' flats. Up and down flights of stairs she went, sometimes sliding down the handrails, putting ordered buns into bags and hanging them outside each apartment. She had to hurry so that she would not be late for school. She was often so exhausted when she got to school that not surprisingly she would fall asleep at her desk. When she was discovered the teacher would send her to stand outside the classroom door. How Marta hated this, especially if someone passed by.

All this just for a few pennies to help Mutti!

The punishment was unjustified in her mind, being tired because she was running her little heart out doing a good turn…

Some of her happiest times at school were spent on the sports field. Marta greatly enjoyed running in the races and her aim was always to be first. She was chosen to be a member of the team to represent her class in inter-school competitions, and this made her very proud. Once a week the class went to an indoor swimming pool to learn to swim. Marta enjoyed this very much, and she took to the water like a duck and was always the last one to come out.

Watching the older girls making beautiful swallow dives from the top of the diving board she decided it looked so easy she would have a go at copying them. Off she went, up the ladder, but as she tiptoed to the end of the board and looked down her heart sank and she felt a queer feeling in her stomach, so she decided to give up the idea of this foolish attempt and turned to go down again. But she was confronted by girls standing behind her, blocking the way down. Rather than lose face Marta stepped slowly forward again. Gaining courage she stretched her arms out and dived…

She was fortunate that she made a reasonable dive. After the initial shock had subsided and her heart had started to beat normally once more she decided to repeat her performance, just to prove she could do it again. It make her feel she had achieved something.

Marta was fascinated by the pictures shown outside the cinema. Going home from school one day, as she turned the corner Marta beheld a frightful sight. Above the entrance to the cinema was a huge, ugly head with big protruding eyes; *Frankenstein*. It was getting dark and the ugly shape was outlined against the building. The big chin was moving up and down and a voice came from the mouth, warning people of a nervous disposition that this was a horror film. The eyes lit up menacingly at the onlookers who were curiously looking at the monstrous head. Marta shuddered and hurried home. She always remembered that advertisement.

Another film which was full of horror and sadness was the true story *The Sinking of the Titanic*. This had a great effect on people, making many of them cry. Saturday afternoon matinees were when Marta went into the cinema. Those were the days when children queued up to see Tom Mix with his clever horse, Rebel the Alsatian and Lassie films. Shirley Temple and Harold Lloyd were among the stars of those days. They were films of great excitement and harmless fun…

A Merry-go-round

ANOTHER SUMMER HOLIDAY HAD STARTED AND MARTA WAS sent by the authorities to a farm for two weeks to put some colour in her cheeks and strength into her meek little body. Marta rejoiced at the notice because it meant being away from the flat.

She rather liked the rural atmosphere and farming people. The couple she stayed with were very nice, but not young any more, and they had a maid looking after the place.

After Marta was shown to the bedroom she was to share with the maid there was a big dinner waiting. During the meal there was talk about a travelling fair that had established itself on the village green and was to stay for a week before moving on to another village. The man volunteered to take Marta along to see the fair. The kind lady gave her some money to spend, but warned her not to spend it all at once. Marta, with shining, bright eyes grateful for all this kindness and thoughtfulness promised to be good. The man holding her hand made her feel very secure in a way.

Arriving at the fair there was music shattering the peace, as each amusement had a different tune and tempo – all very exciting to a child, of course. Marta pointed to a roundabout with seats on chains. 'Could I have a ride?' she pleaded with the man.

How could he refuse? 'All right then,' he consented as he lifted her into a seat and fastened the chair across her front. 'Now keep still,' he warned.

Off they went, round and round, higher and higher, and Marta squealed with delight.

But why is pleasure always short-lived? she wondered, because after a while she was beginning to feel sick. Not long ago she had eaten a big meal.

As the ride came to a halt she shakily got out of her seat and could hardly walk. She was very sick on her way back to the house and was sent straight to bed after a drink.

Well, the strangest thing happened to Marta: some time after she found herself hanging outside a window and at the precise moment of truth she let go and fell onto the garden path below.

A full moon was shining and that helped her to see and she got back into the house through an open door at the side of the house, left open for the maid who was out at that time. Marta crept up the dark stairs so as not to disturb anybody.

Suddenly she sensed something moving behind her. She quickly slipped into the bedroom and straight into the bed, covering herself completely. At the same moment the light was switched on and the maid stood at her bedside. 'Did you get out of your bed, Marta?' she asked.

Marta didn't know what to say to that question, as her eyes stared at the wide-open window. The maid followed her stare.

After a moment of thought Marta started to cry. The maid sat down on the bed, putting her arms around her for comfort. 'Now, now, what's the matter? Tell me,' she persuaded, then she noticed the dirt and dampness on her nightie.

'Whatever has happened to you, Marta?'

In tears Marta told her that she must have been dreaming about being on the roundabout and then as she was trying to get off she found herself hanging outside the window.

'Oh, Marta!' The maid was full of anxiety and pulled away the bedclothes to reveal a very swollen ankle and a grazed arm. She changed her into a clean nightie and cleaned the dirt off her hands and feet. Marta begged her not to tell her kind hosts what had happened. The maid nodded to quieten her down. Next morning there was great commotion. Of course the maid had to tell them and Marta was brought down. Her foot was very swollen and her arm sore.

After she had eaten her breakfast the man took her in a horsetrap to the doctor and he suggested she have an X-ray, so she was taken on a train to a little town nearby. Fortunately nothing was broken, but the best of it was that she was not punished for it, just shown great concern – that was new to her. But at night the window was fastened together with string, just for security.

Despite all this, she still spent a lovely time there.

A Lodger

NOW WAS TO COME A PERIOD OF MARTA'S LIFE WHICH WAS to bring her a lot of unhappiness and bewilderment. Hans was very grown up at fifteen years old. When he left school he was sent away to a household of farming people to be looked after with good food and to learn a proper trade. It was to give him a fair chance to better himself, or so Mutti was told.

Now there was just Mutti and Marta left in the flat, but not for long. Mutti decided to take in a paying lodger and she soon found one. Marta did not like the look of him at all. He was tall and lean with a haggard face, his eyes were cold and made her shiver. He was a very good cabinetmaker when sober, but was a heavy drinker and the flat became hell.

Soon after he moved in, some nights Marta would be sent by Mutti to a little beer bar across the street to ask him to come home. It was torture for her to enter the local wondering what mood he would be in, because it all depended on how the card game was going for him. Sometimes he would give her some money and be kind to her to please Mutti, but at other times he would become violent, raging and shouting abuse as he swayed across the street, swearing at people as he passed.

But there were even more problems to come. The lodger was a married man who had deserted his wife. He had two grown-up sons. One was a ruffian like his father and eventually ended up in prison. The other son was the total opposite; gentle and likeable. He was very good-looking, with jet black hair and large, soulful eyes like his mother. Not surprisingly he married a very beautiful girl, but they had nowhere to stay.

Kind-hearted Mutti offered them a room at the flat until they could find somewhere else to live. Marta's bed was moved out of the room into an alcove at the end of a dark passage. Dark curtains screened it, making it airless and claustrophobic. Although this upset Marta, she was consoled by the fact that she liked the young couple and they were kind to her. Beauty of any kind appealed to this child who had to go without so many things in life, and Richard and Kate were certainly a lovely pair.

Shortly after moving in Kate gave birth to a baby girl. Like her father she had curly hair and dark eyes. While this little family lived with them there was peace at the flat most of the time.

They eventually found a place of their own, but their happiness was short-lived. At an early age Richard died of TB leaving Kate a widow and the baby fatherless...

Marta was so embarrassed by the lodger's behaviour that she would keep her distance and pretend she didn't know him. He acted as if he owned the flat, and Marta could not understand why Mutti tolerated the degrading way she was treated. People who lived in the flats above and below them became hostile, complaining about the noise. They even reported what was going on to the rent man but no action was taken.

After school Marta always made sure she did not arrive home until Mutti was there. How sad that she was afraid to be in her own home now! This was a time when the strong bond between Mutti and herself seemed to weaken. Marta felt bewildered and lost. To kill time, on her way home from school Marta started to explore the various streets she passed and lingered outside the cinema, gazing at the pictures displayed outside. Even further afield was a plot of disused land where she discovered a pool of water in the deep hollow of a large mound of earth. There she spent hours trying to catch newts in a glass jar.

One day as she made her way home she became aware that an Alsatian dog was following her. Most children of her age would have been afraid of such a big dog, but not Marta. Her love and trust of animals was so deep that it didn't even occur to her that the dog might be unfriendly if approached. She stopped and put her arms around his neck.

'Are you lost?' she asked, looking into the dog's eyes as if in her child-like way she expected an answer.

The dog looked at her with the same pleading eyes as if asking her to let him stay with her. He trotted beside her all the way to the flat. No one was there, so Marta sat down on the stairway with this huge Alsatian next to her. She was stroking it lovingly when Mutti arrived home. She stopped in surprise at seeing her daughter sitting there with the dog.

'What are you doing with that dog? Where did it come from and who does it belong to?'

'I don't know,' Marta replied. 'He followed me home. Please can I keep him?'

Mutti looked at her as if she hadn't heart right. 'Of course you can't! Take him to the police station right away.'

Marta knew that it was no good arguing, so she sadly took the dog and set off for the police station. 'Grown-ups have no hearts,' she told him, as they slowly walked along.

The policeman at the desk of the station said, 'So you found this dog, then?'

'Oh no,' Marta replied, 'he found me, but my mother will not let me keep him…'

'Very sensible,' he said, as he tried to get hold of the dog. 'Run along home, then. I'll take care of him now.'

Looking back, Marta saw the dog struggling to free itself so that it could go with her again. She ran all the way home, sobbing as she did so, thinking about all the people who had no hearts.

As she lay in her bed that night she tried in her childish way to think of a way out of her problems, but as morning dawned nothing had changed…

A Passing

A DAY WHICH MARTA WOULD ALWAYS REMEMBER WAS WHEN death first affected her young life. Coming home from school one day she was met by her anxious-looking step-grandfather (a meek little man who always seemed to be in the shadow of his wife). He told her to run to the school where Mutti was cleaning and fetch her home immediately. Apparently Grandma was very ill. Marta felt that something awful was going to happen, so she ran as fast as possible. If she had only had some money she could have used a tram!

On reaching the school, (which was a new senior school, not the one she had been to previously), she had no idea where to find Mutti, so she ran through the corridors calling her name.

'Mutti, where are you?' she shouted, and was glad to hear Mutti's familiar voice answering.

'What are you doing here?' she asked Marta.

'Granddad sent me to fetch you home,' she panted, 'Grandma is very ill, she had a stroke,' she added.

'Oh my God!' Mutti went pale.

Mutti hurried to find someone who would take over her work and wasted no time putting on her coat.

Arriving back home Mutti told Marta to go to the flat while she went into Grandma's flat.

Marta waited anxiously for Mutti to come home, but it was some time before she came through the door, red-eyed from weeping. She didn't say much to Marta, but there seemed an eerie chill in the atmosphere to the sensitive child.

Uncle Heini came across later to tell Mutti that there was no hope for their mother. The stroke had been a massive one and it was just a matter of time. In a very short time she had passed away, gone from their lives for ever.

Mutti went into mourning for a long time, as was the tradition in those days. The black clothes accentuated her pale, distressed face. At forty-five her hair was already turning grey. She looked old for her age, but it was not surprising; all she had known in her life was hard work and no security.

A Serious Occasion

THE YEAR 1936 WAS A MILESTONE IN MARTA'S LIFE. Schooldays were over and Palm Sunday was her confirmation day. Mutti and Marta had made a big effort, and the flat was nice and clean. The curtains looked fresh as the spring sunshine filtered into the room; her own room, just for herself...

Brother Hans had come home for this special occasion. He looked smart and well cared for. He fussed over Marta like a father, making sure her hands and fingernails were not their usual dirty colour. Mutti took great pride in buying a beautiful, deep blue silk dress for Marta to wear in the traditional fashion of that time. She looked with admiration at her daughter. The ugly duckling had grown into a shapely teenager. Her long red hair shone after all the brushing done by Hans. Suddenly Marta herself felt grown up, as if the child-like fantasies with animals as companions in her innocent dream world had come to an end...

'Come along now, we must go,' Mutti's voice broke into her thoughts.

Looking at her mother, Marta thought how smart she looked in a new outfit. As they linked arms with Hans in the middle they all felt that this was a proud moment.

They made their way to the church with a feeling of happiness. It was the first time Marta had seen the inside of this church. The cool, dim atmosphere was in great contrast to the sunny day outside.

With a solemn face she joined the other girls already waiting there. She felt nervous and occupied herself looking at the stained glass windows where the rays of sunlight were filtering through. The organ started to play and a hush swept through the congregation. The pastor appeared and started preaching.

After the singing and blessing the girls walked past their parents and friends down the aisle with tense, solemn faces, but once outside they started to relax, relieved that it was all over.

After the congregation had left the church they and the newly confirmed girls dispersed to their own homes.

When Marta arrived back at the flat she was delighted by neighbours sending flowers or a little gift with a card of congratulations. The flat soon became like a flower show and little baskets of violets and posies of spring flowers. The new 'Miss' loved all this attention. With her new status came the prospect of finding a job and getting paid for it. Yes, this was a new beginning…

Hans was learning the trade of tailoring. However, he was enlisted into the army. When he came home on leave Marta thought how smart he looked in his uniform. Always neat and particular about his appearance, he looked immaculate.

'You look smashing,' Marta remarked to him.

He accepted the compliment, hugging her.

After the happy greetings were over he changed from his uniform into a training suit which he had made himself before joining the army. Marta also noticed that he placed his trousers under the mattress of his bed to keep the crease perfect.

Living for years amid the chaos of Mutti' untidiness had obviously not affected this young man.

Mutti cooked his favourite meal of pork, red cabbage and potatoes. After they had eaten they enjoyed a cosy family reunion with Hans playing his Waldzitta, while Mutti and Marta sang along with him to old folk songs.

What a lovely time the happy trio enjoyed for a short while. Fortunately, the lodger was playing cards somewhere so he didn't cast a blight on the evening.

Boy Meets Girl

It was a novelty to Marta to be able to enjoy life in a new and independent way. After working and getting paid for it, there was an opportunity to pursue her greatest pleasure: dancing. On Sunday afternoons, tea dances were held in a café quite near to where she lived. With a school friend she decided to venture into this new territory...

Marta pushed her friend through the door to go first. She followed shyly behind. Quickly they found a little table with two empty chairs. The sound of the music got into Marta's body and she wanted to dance, but had to sit and wait for someone to ask her to partner him.

Sipping her apple juice she tried to appear casual when a tall lad came up to their table. He bowed towards Marta, 'May I have this dance, please?' he asked her politely.

She could have jumped for joy, but didn't let him see that she was excited. He put his arm around her waist and guided her among the dancers onto the floor, swaying to the music; '*Roter Mohn*' (Red Polly) – a very popular tune. Marta dared not look at his face, instead she watched other people's faces and their varying expressions.

When the dance was over her partner escorted her to the table and with a 'thank you' he turned away.

After a few visits to the café Marta became more aware of the faces of some of the opposite sex – one in particular, but he had a girlfriend with him.

A few weeks later the unexpected happened: he came over to their table. Marta's heart started to play up. *Who is he going to ask for a dance?* she wondered.

It was her he wanted! She blushed and felt quite dizzy with excitement as they made their way onto the dance floor. At the end of another dance together he asked if he could see her home. Shyly, Marta nodded. She usually refused such offers because it was the dancing she came for, not the boys, but this one was different.

His name was Peter. He was very nice and they talked about lots of various things as they walked along. They kissed in a harmless way and parted with a promise to see each other again.

This platonic type of friendship went on for a while, and Marta mentioned to him one day that there was to be a dance for all the girls who had recently finished school. He agreed to accompany her, but Marta was not so sure about revealing he was her boyfriend just in case one of her old school friends tried to take him away from her, so she suggested meeting him inside the dance hall.

As they went into the dance hall greeting old classmates, Gerda nudged Marta to notice that most of the other girls wore long, satin dresses in bright colours. They felt quite plain in their simple outfits.

It crossed Marta's mind; *What chance do I stand against these dolly birds?* She need not have worried – she was straight away asked to dance and was not a wallflower like some of those in their expensive dresses. It was while she was dancing that she noticed Peter had arrived looking very smart. He scanned the crowd for Marta.

As soon as the dance was over she went up to him and for the rest of the evening they stayed together.

The following week the last school meeting was held. Marta was not well and did not attend. When Gerda came to visit her she hold Marta, 'You should have heard them, the girls, talking about you and Peter!'

'What about us?' Marta queried.

'Well, they wondered how you managed to get hold of such a good-looking chap. They also wondered what on earth he saw in you, making suggestive remarks that you are not as naïve as you are made out to be.'

Marta was furious. *They always see the worst in people, never their virtues*, she thought. But there was a certain satisfaction in thinking that they were so obviously jealous…

However, the unexpected happened: the young romance ended without warning. The next time Marta arrived at the café

Peter was there, but he had found a new girlfriend and was dancing with her. She felt quite hurt at the way he had acted and went home. For several weeks she did not go near the café, but then she came to the conclusion that she would go and show him that he was not the only one for her. It really hadn't been serious enough to be heartbroken about it. Such is the way of life. There was a great deal more to learn about relationships – this was only the beginning...

A New Power

POLITICAL UNREST EMERGED EVERYWHERE AS HITLER BEGAN his rise to power. In the streets arguments between people of different beliefs were becoming common. The young will always lend an ear to the rallying cry of a new cause, and soon the Hitler Youth Movement emerged. Their uniform made them feel important. Marta avoided these new activities because she was afraid of any disturbance or violence – it was bad enough trying to find a peaceful existence at home, now there seemed little peace in the streets. She would often hear marching music and see boys strutting along. There were fights sometimes between the youth in uniform and those who did not agree with what the Hitler Youth stood for. Promises of the good life were continually announced over the radio: *Es ensteht das dritte Reich* (the creation of the third Reich)…

Amidst this unrest Marta's life was suddenly changed for her: a new law was passed, and all girls were to attend a six-month course to make them useful citizens of the Reich. They were to be sent to camps for a period of time and so they had to leave their places of employment.

April 1936 saw about ninety girls from all walks of life gathered at a meeting place and taken by bus away from their weeping parents to an unknown destination in the countryside. This was the first time that Marta would be away from Mutti for such a long spell. She herself was not worried, but felt very sad for her mother as her lonely figure faded out of sight.

The journey was a pleasant drive through the countryside until the bus went up a drive and stopped in front of a large, imposing hall set among trees. The girls and their luggage were quickly unloaded and the bus soon departed.

Out of the main door of the hall came seven stern-looking ladies in uniforms similar to those worn by girl guides. Orders were immediately given for the girls to line up in order of size.

Marta was bundled about like a ball until she finally came to rest at the very end. The fourteen tallest girls were put in the charge of one of the seven leaders, who ordered, 'Pick up your cases and follow me!' The rest of the girls were sorted into similar groups, each with a leader in command. They were then led through a long passage into a large, open hall. A wide staircase led from this up to the landings and numerous bedrooms. Tin lockers were standing along the landings and each girl was allocated one of these for her belongings.

There were six bunk beds in the bedroom Marta was to share with her companions. The girls looked depressed, there wasn't enough room to swing a cat. However, there was nothing they could do about it so they decided to toss for which beds they would have; this would prevent quarrels. Marta ended up with the top bunk in the middle of the room, not the best position to be in...

Camp Life

JUST AS MARTA WAS GETTING TO KNOW THE GIRL IN THE NEXT bed to her, there was a shrill whistle through a loudspeaker above their heads and a voice announced that they were to assemble immediately in the hall downstairs.

They all hurried down and each group was told to stand in a line facing their leader. Another lady then appeared – she was in command of the camp. In a brusque voice she informed them that the aim of their six-month stay in the camp was to teach them discipline and orderliness at all times and to make them useful citizens and a credit to their homeland. The girls listened intently, naturally apprehensive of this strange new life that had been thrust upon them.

After this they were led into a large dining room. *Food at last*, thought Marta – she felt so hungry!

After a nice meal the girls were free to pack their belongings in the lockers and to get to know each other. At nine p.m. they had to prepare for bed, and at ten p.m. it was lights out. Marta was so tired she fell asleep quickly.

This is where years of having to be self-reliant helped her. Some of the other girls who had been much luckier in their home lives and had everything made easy for them cried themselves to sleep.

At six the following morning, the bedroom door flew open and the piercing blast of a whistle woke the sleeping girls, frightening them to death. While they were trying to gather their senses, a loud voice commanded, 'Strip your beds and be downstairs in ten minutes for PT!' What a scramble the first morning!

PT consisted of running around the estate for half an hour, followed by deep breathing exercises. After that they had to wash themselves in an old washhouse outside the hall. No warm water was available – just cold taps with small wash bowls underneath.

Now – wait for it – the girls had to strip naked! This caused a few blushes among them, especially when their leader did the same! In those days there was no sex education and most girls of that age were somewhat naïve, so this was quite a shock to them. After the initial embarrassment, the girls soon changed their attitude and found it a natural thing to do. (They hadn't any choice in the matter, anyhow.) They ended up throwing water over one another and having great fun.

After this they hurried upstairs to tidy themselves and make their beds. As soon as this was done more orders came over the loud speaker: they had to assemble in the hall and then march outside while the flag was hoisted and then await inspection.

Breakfast was at eight, and the thought of lovely food as they wound their way to the dining room made the girls hurry to their allotted places at the big tables.

What a shock to most of the girls when they saw what breakfast consisted of! It was a dish of milk pudding, a breakfast bun with a pat of butter and a drink of tea or milk. To Marta this was good, regular food and she was happy whatever the offering.

After breakfast the girls had quite a surprise because they were told to queue up in front of a little counter in a storage room where they would be issued with kit for their stay at the camp. Two ladies behind the counter asked each girl her bust, waist and hip measurements. Quickly sorting out a pile of garments, they handed them over the counter with a list of the items on top. The girls then had to sign for them. Marta could hardly carry the bulky pile upstairs!

In the bedroom everyone began inspecting the issue. Holding the various clothes up in front of them, there was a lot of giggling and exclamation at how they looked.

'A dress for working in – very chic,' one girl remarked, 'especially the length! Definitely the latest fashion…'

Next came a skirt, blouse and tie similar to the ones the leaders wore. There were thick socks and boots with studs on the soles.

'Oh, these boots were made for walking…' quoted one wit. The remarks going around would probably not have amused the leaders! The tracksuit did not come in for any criticism, as it was good quality, light and warm and a real asset for outdoor activity. Blankets, rucksacks and camping gear were also issued. For all these items the girls were held responsible. There was a kit inspection every weekend, and woe betide anyone who had lost anything! There was a lot of cleaning and polishing before these inspections. It was, in fact, very like army life.

Every week several girls from each group were selected to work together. One week it would be housework, another week kitchen duties. After that would come gardening and farming. They would all change about so that everyone had thorough training in all aspects. All this was done under supervision, of course. Some lucky girls were selected to work on farms outside the estate, and this was considered a privilege as it was a more relaxed atmosphere than the military one of the camp.

One of the girls chosen to work on the outside farms was Hanne. She slept in the bunk next to Marta, and they immediately struck up a friendship which was to last for the rest of their lives. Hanne was a fun-loving girl, and Marta wished that she had been chosen to work on the outside farms with her.

After a few weeks of the tough army-style discipline the girls learned what it was all about and what to expect. They dreaded the weekend kit inspection, standing watching the leaders examining every single thing. They even used a long nail to scrape around the boots to see if any dirt had been left there. The girls were awarded points for all their work, efforts and for the results of the kit inspections. The idea of this was to find the elite of this course, so the girls tried their hardest to get as many points as possible.

At night the leader would inspect the lockers while the girls were in bed. As they lay there, listening and hoping all was well, the piercing sound of a girl's name would sometimes echo around the dark bedroom. The unfortunate victim would scramble from her bed to find all her clothes scattered on the floor. The leader watched as she tidily folded them up and put them back in her locker. They soon got the message: there was to be no fooling around at this camp…

A Night March

AFTER THE EVENING MEAL THEY HAD A LITTLE TIME FOR leisure to write home, read or whatever they liked to do. Come nine o'clock they were all ready for bed, only too pleased to rest after the hectic day of camp life.

One night after lights out one of the girls started telling a joke. Before long they were all in fits of laughter. 'Hush! Not so loud!' someone warned, indicating the dividing wall between their bedroom and their leader's. 'She will hear us if we make so much noise!' That only made matters worse, and in due course the door flew open.

Klara, the leader, stood there, grim-faced. 'Silence immediately!' she commanded, and stormed back into her bedroom.

Unfortunately, as is often the case with a fit of the giggles, the girls tried hard to stifle their merriment but just couldn't. At that the door flew open again and a nightmare began.

'Get up, make your beds, put on your outdoor clothes and be downstairs in ten minutes,' was the barked command.

They scrambled around like little ants to obey, and were soon downstairs with their overcoats and boots on. What was going to happen, they all wondered, scared by the look on their leader's face.

'Forward march in silence,' she ordered.

Into the night they went, through a dark wood. It was an hour before she brought them to a halt back at the camp. She then told them to stand to attention while she went inside.

Coming out ten minutes later, she said, 'Go back to bed now, and let that be a lesson to you!'

Sure enough, it did not happen again.

There was a brighter side of camp life at times; it was rather fun in a way.

They were told that everyone had to undergo a test of courage. Klara explained that one night they would be sleeping in a tent, and each girl in turn would be on watch outside for an hour. Being the type of person she was, Klara chose a place in a large park where she knew there were pigs and boars roaming free. She intended her group to have a real test of courage!

After pitching the tents underneath some trees, the girls tossed for their various times on watch. Marta's time was midnight. *Now is the hour*, she thought, as she crept out of the tent.

She decided to climb onto the thick branch of a nearby tree. This seemed a secure outlook to tomboy Marta.

After a short while she could just about make out some shapes as they moved about in the darkness. Then one ventured very close to the tent, as if to inspect it... So Marta threw a branch at the creature below and made it move on.

The Mascot

AS MARTA WAS THE SMALLEST GIRL IN THE CAMP THE OTHERS decided to make her their mascot and to nickname her Mickey (after Mickey Mouse, who was very popular at that time). It didn't worry her – she actually enjoyed being a friendly mascot.

Shortly after the test of courage incident Marta was chosen for some reason to accompany group No. 1 on their night out in a tent. It was pitched in an open field, and Marta didn't have to watch outside during the night this time. She had just settled down for a good night's sleep, when without warning all hell let loose. The leader looked outside to see what was happening.

All around were figures covered by white sheets, banging something hidden underneath them. They were gradually coming closer. The girls had nothing to defend themselves with, and taking a look at all their petrified faces the leader turned to Marta and said, 'You are small and quite agile; see if you can get through to the camp for help.' She pushed Marta outside, giving her no chance to refuse. 'Hurry, now!' were the words of command Marta heard as she crawled on all fours through the wet grass towards the camp.

Suddenly she froze: a big, dark shape was looming near, and a snorting sound sent a shiver of fear through her as she realised it was a big Friesian bull, a fearful creature.

Too late for praying, she thought, *just run for it, my girl*!

The lights from the camp were beckoning her through the trees, and the noise behind was urging her on. With an extra spurt she reached the fence and hastily squeezed through. She heard her blouse tear and something warm running down her arm, but she carried on undaunted to reach the camp.

After raising the alarm some of the leaders, with volunteers, armed themselves with brooms or whatever was handy and went off to rescue the damsels in distress. Marta was taken into the kitchen, looking as if she had been in a battle herself. There was blood oozing out of her torn blouse and she was covered in mud. A leader looked after her and soon she was in bed and fast asleep, tired out after all her exertions.

Next day there was a lot of excitement in the camp about the previous night's incident. Everyone was talking about what had happened. The story was that some of the young fellas in the neighbourhood had heard about the 'tent night' and had gathered together to scare the girls off. Instead they were beaten off when the reinforcements arrived, thanks to Marta! Another test of courage passed with flying colours…

A Cat's Dilemma

ONE WARM DAY MARTA WAS DETAILED TO WORK OUTSIDE chopping wood. There she caught sight of a wild cat under a pile of logs. When she cautiously approached it she realised it was injured. She saw that it had what looked like a shotgun wound.

'Oh, you pool little creature!' she cried as she tried to stroke it and to see just how badly it was hurt. Any sudden move on her part startled the poor thing. Marta had to go for the afternoon break. She begged the girl in charge for some milk and a dish to put it in for the unfortunate cat.

'All right, then,' she pushed a little jar into Marta's jacket pocket to hide it. 'Don't get caught, or we shall be in trouble.'

'Okay,' Marta said, 'thank you very much.'

She hurried back to the place where she had left it, but there was no cat to be seen. After she had started working again she spotted movements near another pile of wood a short distance away. Making no sudden movements she put the milk on the floor, calling softly, *Muschi, Muschi*. The cat approached very cautiously, and then lapped up the nourishing milk. As if to say thank you she sat for a while licking her paws, and then disappeared from sight again.

Marta was happy with this success, but doubted the cat could survive because of the injury. All the same she saved a scrap of food from her next meal and when no one was looking deposited it underneath the pile of wood.

The next day she was eager to see if the food had gone. It had, but she did not see the cat again for two weeks. She thought it must have died from its injury, but kept putting out scraps just in case it was the cat taking them and not some other animal.

One day she heard meowing coming from an outbuilding, and there was the cat, looking very thin but with the wound dried up and healing to a certain extent.

'Oh, you poor creature!' Marta cried with great compassion. She put some scraps down, but the cat started to behave unusually. It seemed to Marta that as the cat was calling out to something in the darkness, to her surprise she heard a faint reply from inside the building! Cautiously she moved to the opening, and looking in she could see four tiny kittens in the dim interior.

'I will get you some more milk,' she promised the cat, 'no matter how difficult in will be.'

In the kitchen she poured out her story and every girl was ready to help such a moving cause. They asked Marta continually about the cat and her kittens after her frequent visits to take food and milk to them because she asked them not to go in themselves in case it frightened the cat away. The little family thrived thanks to Marta's concern about their welfare and the cooperation of the other girls. Another good deed done.

The Happy Wanderers

MARTA'S NEXT ADVENTURE WAS A HOLIDAY. 'THESE BOOTS were made for walking' could have been the theme song for the week ahead.

Plans had been made for a trip into Schleswig Holstein. Each girl had a pack on her back containing a blanket, cooking utensils and a minimum change of clothes. ...*Have pack, will travel!*... So they set off, singing at the tops of their voices as they marched through the countryside.

But after a time, many of the girls were complaining about sore feet and aching backs. Sleeping on hard beds at various hostels or camping out did not improve their spirits. Only the really fit girls enjoyed this trek through villages and little fishing ports, and Marta and Hanne were two of them, sitting on the quayside eating fresh shrimps straight off the boats coming in.

After a week the Chicken Group (as they were called) returned to the camp so that another group could go away.

The last episode in the schedule of the camp was a song contest. With the competitive secrecy of this came great fun in trying to find a place to practice so no one could hear their song before the final show, and they had to be good.

They never would have believed it, but Marta and Hanne actually won the contest with their song, '*Spatzen Conzert*'!

It was a thrilling experience for all concerned.

By now the time was running out and the end of this trial in view. Parents were invited to the passing out parade. This was to enable them to talk to the leaders and find out how their daughters had come through the experience. The Chicken Group came a close second on points to the elite, and felt very proud of their achievement. Even Klara, their leader, seemed pleased with their success together.

So ended a time well spent; as far as Marta and Hanne were concerned it meant the start of a beautiful friendship, to last all through their lives.

Mutti was so pleased to see her daughter again! She had missed her little nestling and it was understandable; Marta was all she had left of a family. Hugging each other they boarded the bus for home.

The homecoming was pleasant. The flat was tidy, and as Marta walked into the sitting room she noticed that quite some changes had taken place. There was a big, round, polished table with a veneered star centrepiece (Marta had an eye for beautiful things). Also new was a big bookcase made by the lodger who was a cabinetmaker by trade. A newly acquired gramophone stood in one corner, a luxury bought on HP. Marta was warned not to touch it.

Land Army

THE PROPAGANDA OF HITLER'S PARTY WAS SEEN ON POSTERS everywhere and heard frequently over the radio. One item of news which caught Marta's attention was about girls working on farms for one year. It seemed a good idea to her after the experiences at the camp, so she spoke to Hanne about it. They had kept in contact with each other after returning home from the camp.

Off they went to the Labour Exchange to find out more about it. They were told it would come into force in the spring. 'If we volunteered early, would we be able to get a place close to each other?' they enquired.

'We will do our best,' the person in authority answered.

April saw Marta and Hanne aboard a train on their way to yet another assignment. Station after station girls were disembarking at their destinations. The two friends were getting anxious, but at last they arrived at the place they were looking for.

'Here we are,' said Hanne, and picking up their cases they stepped out onto the platform of a little station. They looked around for the farmers who were supposed to be picking them up. A couple approached asking for Hanne. 'Come along, then. We will take you to our farm.'

Hanne looked at Marta's bewildered face.

'What about my friend?' she desperately asked the couple.

'What about her?' the couple answered impatiently.

'We were promised we would be working close together,' said Hanne.

Marta looked around, but there was no one else on the deserted platform. There was no one to meet her. She sat down on her suitcase, tears rolling down her cheeks.

Nothing ever seemed to be straight forward for her. *The devil seems very fond of putting a damper on my plans*, she thought. *What shall I do now?*

The farmer was quite prepared to just leave her there, but his wife felt sorry for her.

'How about Marien Hof?' she suggested to her husband. 'We cannot leave the poor girl here!'

'We can have a try,' he grumbled, not very pleased at being troubled with this extra girl.

There was a pony and trap for transport. The farmer lifted the girls' cases up and told them to sit at the back end with their legs dangling down. The pony trotted along a bumpy track, bouncing Marta and Hanne up and down, but they didn't notice the discomfort because they were too upset about the distressing situation poor Marta was in.

'What if they don't take you on?' asked Hanne. 'I am not staying either,' she muttered. They dared not think about what might happen.

A passing farmer shouted, 'Nice little piggies you got there, Albert!'

The two girls blushed at this remark.

The cart swung into a big yard and there was Marien Hof, a large farmhouse with the name in large letters over the entrance. The farmer and his wife disappeared into the house, leaving the girls sitting there with dangling legs and heavy hearts. The time seemed endless as they sat there, silent and tense.

At last there was movement at the door of the farmhouse. The couple Hanne was going to came out followed by an elderly couple who looked very severe.

'Oh no, Marta!' Hanne said, gripping her hand tightly. Hanne's farmer lifted Marta from the cart and asked, 'Which is your case?'

Speechless, she pointed to it and he lifted it down and joined his wife, who had already climbed up onto the pony cart. Waving, they trotted out of the yard and out of sight, leaving Marta apprehensive about this new development.

Marien Hof

THE ELDERLY COUPLE LOOKED AT HER, NOT TOO PLEASED by this unexpected intrusion. To them she didn't look strong enough to cope with heavy farm work. They had yet to find out that appearances aren't always what they seem...

The man picked up Marta's suitcase and walked back into the house. Wearily she followed him, wondering what life had in store for her this time.

Inside the farmhouse the man shouted, 'Hilde!' a door opened and a girl of colossal size appeared, filling the whole doorway.

'Hilde!' the farmer said to her, 'take this girl to your room.'

Marta followed the girl up some stairs, through a passage and into a nice comfortable bedroom. Two beds and a wardrobe were the only furniture in there. Hilde put the case on a bed. 'This is yours,' she commented, looking at Marta's small figure with something akin to amusement.

'What's your name?' she enquired.

'Marta,' was the rather nervous reply.

'Where do you come from?'

Just as Marta told her that she came from Hamburg, there was a call from below telling them to come downstairs. Hilde led the way into a large kitchen. There was a huge stove in a corner and a long table with benches on each side. This was Hilde's domain, and she was told by the farmer's wife to get the supper ready.

The serious-faced farmer beckoned Marta to have a look around the farm. She felt cold, but obediently followed him outside. They went through a door into stables where to Marta's delight she saw three horses. Her eyes lit up and her fears seemed to disappear.

'Can I stroke one?' she asked the man.

'No,' he brusquely replied. 'They are very tired after working in the fields and two of them are having foals very shortly.'

Marta was disappointed but understood, and she kept still so that she would not disturb them.

The tour then went through another door into the cowshed. It was well set out with a central pathway for feeding time.

On either side were a dozen stalls for the milking cows. Each had a name above it. Nearby were the calves' pens and in a corner was a pile of turnips. Everything was very tidy and clean.

After the work had been explained to Marta they returned to the kitchen, where the delicious smell of bacon made her realise how hungry she was. She was told where to sit at the table, and at that moment a young man walked in. Taking off his cap he walked to the sink and washed his hands and then sat down at the table.

Big plates of steaming food were served by Hilde. The two men were given preference, followed by the farmer's wife and Marta. Then Hilde put her own plate on the table and sat down next to Marta. The farmer then explained her presence to the young man, who had looked rather surprised to see a strange young girl sitting at the table. He smiled at her and she found herself blushing as she smiled back.

After the meal Marta helped to clear the table and wash up. When all was finished Hilde asked her if she would like to have another look around.

'Yes, I would,' she replied, glad to escape from the attention of the others.

As they stepped outside an Alsatian which she hadn't seen before growled a warning. Being Marta it did not enter her head to be afraid. She spoke quietly and calmly to him and he sensed that here was a friend.

'What's his name?' she asked Hilde. His name was Lord, and he was a friend worth having.

Marta thought of the Alsatian which she had wanted to keep so much and which Mutti did not approve of.

She had often wondered what had happened to him after leaving him at the police station.

She asked Hilde the name of the couple who had taken her in, and also that of the young man. No one had bothered to tell her as yet. She was told that they were Herr and Frau Muller, and did not own Marien Hof but managed it for a solicitor working in a nearby town. The young man was called Karl and was the farm labourer.

That night Marta was so tired she fell asleep almost as soon as her head touched the pillow.

Rural Freedom

AT FIVE THIRTY IN THE MORNING CAME THE CALL FOR HILDE and Karl to start their busy working day. When Hilde had dressed and gone downstairs, Marta lay thinking of the events of the previous day. She wondered how Hanne was getting on and hoped she would see her friend soon. Also, how long would she herself be allowed to stay at Marien Hof?

At seven o'clock she went downstairs. Shyly she entered the kitchen. Hilde was busy making breakfast, as Marta sat at the table, enjoying the appetising smell of home-baked bread as she did so. *Mmm, this is wonderful*, she thought.

After everyone had eaten a hearty breakfast the farmer discussed with Karl what work was to be done. He hold him to take Marta to one of the fields to help with the muck spreading. The two of them went outside and Karl hitched one of the horses to the cart, which was already full of manure, and after telling Marta to get up onto the seat beside him, they trotted out of the yard.

Arriving at the field, he put a fork into her hand and told her how to spread the muck about – no modern machines in those days. At last she felt useful. She was doing a job; it didn't matter what it entailed. She was willing to do her share. It boosted her ego.

It was a day well spent, despite the hard work as far as she was concerned.

She was very tired and more than ready for bed at nine o'clock. *This is the life for me*, she thought as she drifted into a deep, contented sleep.

Milking was done by hand in those days. The milk would be put into large cans through filters which Karl put on a platform outside the farm gate to be picked up by transport from a large dairy that bought most of their milk. Marta was eager to learn how to milk, so Herr Muller showed her how to do so. He pointed out a cow which he thought would be suitable for her to have a try on. It came easily to her, and she turned out to be a natural and soon she increased to six cows, milking each morning and evening. But one thing she found rather hard to do; she had to thoroughly wash the heavy churns in soda water, and found them difficult to handle, but never the less did the job well. An inspector came each week to check on the quality and purity of the milk, so everything had to be scrupulously clean.

There were no more remarks now about being skinny and weak! All the work in the fresh air, sound sleep and of course plenty of good food was having a remarkable effect on Marta; she was gradually turning into a shapely young woman, but she did not seem to realise this. Her mind was still very childlike in many ways.

After a week of learning about the running of the farm and showing what a hard worker she was, Herr Muller became a little more approachable. He was impressed with her special way with animals, too. This young city girl who had been foisted on them was turning out to be a treasure to have about the place…

One day she dared to ask him, 'Where is my friend staying, Herr Muller?'

He pointed at some buildings behind some trees, not very far away. 'There it is. After milking on Sunday go and see her.'

'Thank you,' Marta said, thinking to herself, *This is great progress.*

She set off on Sunday, eager to tell Hanne all about her achievements of the past week.

When she eventually found her friend, she could see that all was not well. The usually happy-go-lucky Hanne looked haggard. She had two small children in her care, and the farmer's wife kept calling her to do some job or other. Marta felt so sorry for her, and realised how lucky she had been to be accepted at Marien Hof so she was glad to go back there.

God works in mysterious ways, she thought, recalling how downhearted she had felt when no one had arrived to meet her at the station that day.

Riding for Pleasure

ONE BEAUTIFUL SUNDAY MORNING, AFTER MILKING MARTA went out into the yard and saw two mares tied up outside without the foals. Karl was putting a saddle on Lotti.

'Where are you going?' Marta asked him.

'To a stud,' Karl answered without looking round at her.

'Can I ride with you?' she enquired.

'It isn't a place for a girl to be present,' he answered, looking a bit embarrassed. Then, seeing how disappointed she looked, he said, 'Go and ask Herr Muller, see what he says.'

She needed no more prompting to do so and hurried into the house. To her surprise, permission was granted on the condition that she did not enter the stud farm; she must stay and wait for Karl outside the gate.

In her innocence she didn't understand the meaning of all this or why. Blissfully happy to go for a ride, it didn't spoil the fun that she had to ride Polly, who was a heavy kind of a mixture. Quiet and docile, she had an unfortunate fault in her hind quarter and it was not a smooth ride. But who cared? Here was a horse, a shining chestnut, and Marta was going to ride on it.

She rode Polly bareback and followed Karl into the lane through the open countryside. This was bliss – a dream come true for Marta.

She tried to get Karl to trot the horses, but he insisted that it was too hot and the horses would start sweating. He was very concerned that this should not happen.

After an hour they approached a large farm.

'Here we are,' said Karl as he dismounted to help Marta off her horse. Taking Polly's reins he led the two mares through a gate.

'Wait here,' he told her.

She watched him disappearing behind some buildings. It seemed ages before he reappeared. He handed Polly's reins back to her, but said that they had to lead the horses for a time instead of riding them.

They walked for quite a distance before Karl lifted Marta back up onto the mare's back, and even then they rode the rest of the way at walking pace.

Before going to bed that night Marta slipped into Polly's stable and stroked the horse to thank it for a super experience.

Working the Season

SUMMER WAS A BUSY TIME AND WITH ALL THE OUTDOOR activity Marta acquired a golden tan. She was happy working with the animals, especially the horses. Karl was very pleased with the way she handled them all.

The cows were put out to grass, and whenever the milking was done in the fields the milk churns were transported on a trolley as the field was not very far from the farm. Marta was delighted to find that the cows came to Karl and herself when called by their names.

Two foals were born during this time and Marta was so pleased when Herr Muller took her in to see them. The horses on the farm were not heavy horses like the ones belonging to the coal merchant in Hamburg, they looked more like riding hacks. Even so, they had to work very hard in the fields.

Before the hay-making Marta spent day after day on her knees weeding lucerne, row upon row. Tedious, yes, but this time alone with nature had a great influence on her. She felt a freedom and happiness, which were new to her.

One Sunday after the morning milking Herr and Frau Muller, Karl and Hilde set off to go to a wedding, saying they would be back before the next milking. The thought of being alone on the farm quite pleased Marta, so she waited for a while after they had departed and then went to Lord, the chained-up guard dog.

When she released him from his chain he was overjoyed at this unexpected freedom. 'Let's make the most of it.' *Oh, what a wonderful feeling this is*, thought Marta as she played with him. Together they walked to the field where the horses were grazing. Marta was tempted to mount Halle, a dark bay mare, but dare not as she was highly spirited and it may have upset the foal. So instead she took Lord back to the farm and fed him a big dinner. After she had eaten a meal herself she spent the rest of the afternoon lying in the long grass daydreaming until she realised that milking time was near. No one had returned yet, so Marta started getting the trolley ready and made her way to the field. She milked the six cows in her charge and then since no one had returned from the wedding she carried on and milked the rest of the herd. As she sat down to do the last one, Herr Muller arrived, still in his best suit.

'Too late,' Marta proudly announced, 'I have milked them all!'

He didn't believe her and went stripping under some cows to check. He was amazed to think that she had milked twelve cows by herself. They pulled the now-heavy trolley back to the farm, and for the first time Marta saw a smile on the man's face. What a thrill for Marta to hear him telling her achievement to his wife and later Hilde and Karl! They agreed that she could have a lie-in the next morning – a treat greatly appreciated by Marta.

Summer at its best was hay-making time. The weather was lovely and warm and there was the lovely fragrance of hay in the air that Marta loved so much. She really enjoyed the time spent forking the hay over, loving the rustling of the drying hay as she turned it. *The world is a beautiful place, I'm glad to be part of it*, she thought, as she glanced around the golden field. The sun was shining warmly on her bending back.

The time came when they put the hay onto a wagon to be taken back to the farm to store it in the hayloft over the cowshed. Marta was riding on one wagon, and as they rode along she gazed at the pastoral scene around her and the cows, sunning their black and white hides, big brown eyes half closed as they chewed their cud. It was a picture of idle contentment.

These beautiful, hazy days of summer left memories pressed between the pages of her mind.

Marta's Downfall

THRESHING TIME WAS ON THE HORIZON. THIS WAS DONE BY a team of men with an old threshing machine. They went round to all the farmers in the area in turn. The farmer Hanne worked for came to Marien Hof to discuss which days they should have the threshing done. Marta saw a chance and asked if she could go and see her friend. Hanne's farmer agreed. 'Yes, I don't see why not. The children should be in bed by now.'

Marta went to see Herr Muller, asking him if it was all right for her to go, and he said that it was, so off she went.

We haven't seen much of each other after all, she thought as she made her way to the other farm.

Hanne was so pleased to see Marta and took her up to her little bedroom. It looked so bare with just a bed with a straw mattress to sleep on. *Poor Hanne, she is not used to sleeping rough,* Marta thought. As they sat talking there came a shout for Hanne. She went to see why she was wanted. When she came back she explained to Marta that the farmer had a brother who helped him and it was him who wanted them to come down.

'What for?' Marta enquired.

'On, come on! Don't be such a scaredy-cat,' her friend urged.

As they entered the sitting room there were three fellows there, and they were all drinking beer.

'Come on girls,' one of them cheered. 'Have a drink with us.'

Marta refused.

'I don't like the stuff,' she said.

'Oh, come on,' another chap coaxed, producing another bottle. 'It's only wine. We thought city girls were good at drinking!'

Just to be polite the two friends accepted a small glass. They thought it was terrible stuff. It seemed to burn their throats. The two innocents didn't realise that it was in fact strong liquor.

Then the girls were offered chocolates, and by the time they had emptied their glasses Marta found herself sitting on a sofa between two of the young men, who were both trying to get fresh with her.

Outside a thunderstorm could be heard raging. It was dark and eerie in the farmhouse. The men didn't seem to notice what was going on outside, they were too intent on getting their way with the young city girls.

As they kept on filling the glasses Marta began to feel sick. The mixture of drinks, chocolate and the men's horrible breath was having an effect on her. Suddenly a thunderbolt struck the electric pylon outside cutting the lights out as the thunder rolled overhead. At that instant Marta slid under the table while Hanne was busy trying to find a candle and matches.

Lights flickered in the room as she lit one. Hanne held the candle up and looked around for her friend, but all she could see were the two men on the sofa embracing each other.

'Marta,' she gasped, 'where are you?'

'Here,' whispered a voice, and she emerged from under the table with great difficulty.

'Oh, Marta! What's the matter?' Hanne anxiously asked her.

'I am drunk and I feel sick, and want to go back to Marien Hof.'

Looking at the farmer's brother pleadingly, Hanne said, 'Please take her back.'

Luckily for Marta either his better nature won or he realised that he would get into serious trouble when his brother returned. He asked one of the other fellows to help him and between them they dragged her outside. She was a dead weight and they were in no state to take her back really.

The rain had subsided but there were puddles everywhere which could not be avoided. All this added to Marta's misery. That short journey seemed never ending, but finally they stood knocking on the kitchen door. As the door opened Marta vaguely saw some horrified faces. What a sight she presented! A limp shape hanging between the two men, dirty and wet, muttering that she was drunk and felt sick...

'Oh my God!' cried Frau Muller at the sight of Marta.

Herr Muller was the first to act, and Karl was called for to help this unfortunate being upstairs. Marta was crying and trying to apologise for the state she was in, but the retching into a bucket that Karl had brought for her stopped all conversation. She felt so dreadful that she just wanted to die.

By this time Hilde had arrived home after her night off. She took over from Karl, but was not as understanding as he had been. She proclaimed Marta not to be the little innocent she had appeared. Before she could try to say anything in her defence Marta passed out and sleep claimed her for the rest of the night.

Meanwhile, downstairs in the kitchen a discussion was in progress. This was a serious matter that needed clearing up. The farmers were responsible for the girls working for them. Anything wrongly done to their charge would have serious consequences for them with those in authority.

'What happened to Marta?' the fellows were asked sternly. 'Has any indecency taken place?'

'No, no!' they assured him. 'We just had a few drinks and she obviously isn't used to it.'

So Marta was cleared of suspicion and the two men were allowed to go back, but not without being warned not to try anything like that again.

Threshing Day

THE NEXT MORNING FOUND MARTA WITH A BAD HANGOVER, but she had to go about her duties as usual. Milking the cows seemed like pulling lead, and when she went back to the kitchen Frau Muller made her sit down and eat some breakfast although it was the last thing she wanted to do.

'You need it,' she insisted. 'We are threshing today so you will have a hard day ahead of you.'

It was true in every sense of the word – just her luck!

As soon as she had left the kitchen Marta was running behind the building, vomiting the whole lot out again. She felt so weak and weary and found the punishment hard to bear. There was hustle and bustle as the threshing machine arrived in the yard and the team of men prepared for action. Everyone had a job to do.

Fortunately, Marta and Hanne had to carry the chaff to the loft in baskets, and every so often Marta had to disappear to retch her insides out. Her condition could not accurately be described – physically or emotionally on this day, and to make matters worse, she accidentally swayed too close to the driving belt only to be thrown sideway with the lashing force that hit her arm.

The swelling was instantly as the pain shot through her arm. After a bandage was placed around her arm she was fit for more work to be done – there was no question of her being excused.

No peace for the wicked, thought Marta.

After the day's hard work there was still the milking to be done and the churns to be washed. The men had moved into the kitchen for a well-earned feast, and the conversation was loud and jovial. Marta was grateful to collapse exhausted into bed as early as possible.

This day was seen through by sheer willpower and determination on her part.

The next day she was so stiff she could hardly get out of bed, but knew that another day of work lay in front of her and she would have to try and forget her aches and pains.

Five thirty in the morning seemed to come round very quickly, and Frau Muller beckoned her to give Marta a stern lecture. The injustice! She vowed never to touch any alcohol again – her insides just could not handle any abuse of this kind. It was a lesson learnt the hard way!

After this unfortunate episode Marta noticed that there was a change of attitude in her friendship with Karl; he was more attentive to her when they were alone together, but she just pretended not to notice this because she did not want to encourage him.

Marta

Hans

From left to right: Marta, Mutti,
Grandmother (seated), Heinrich,
and Granddad

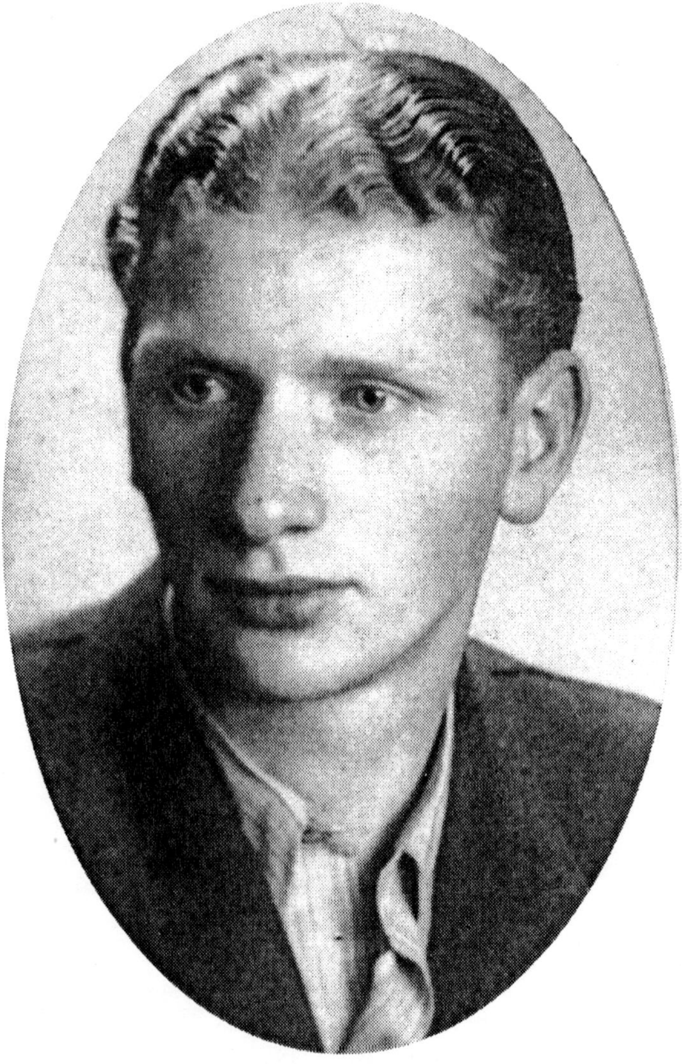

Sister Klara, who killed herself
in 1942

Hans, born 1915,
and Heinrich, born 1919

Marta and Mutti

Hans, Father and Heinrich

Transit Camp

Klara, Father and Marta, 1941

Marta and Hans, 1941

Marta and Karl on their Wedding Day, 1941

Stuart

Potato Picking

THE MORNING DAWNED WHEN POTATO HARVESTING WAS TO begin. A lot of women helpers arrived early at Marien Hof. Everyone seemed full of excitement, and there was a lot of chattering together before they started work. It must have been the thought of extra cash that made them so cheerful, because potato picking is a hard task, not a pleasant one.

A long wagon was already standing in the yard with Polly in harness. Herr Muller ordered plenty of sacks to be put on it and then the women sat along the edges and off they went to the potato field. Karl followed behind with the potato spinner.

When they arrived at the field each woman had a patch to clear after the spinner had gone up the row bringing the potatoes to the surface. They had to be ready to pick the other side of their patch as the spinner came back down.

It was a back-breaking job, and although she was young and fit Marta soon began to ache terribly. Not wanting to show any weakness, she gritted her teeth and kept up with the spinner, filling the sacks on the edge of her patch. The other women ahead eased their chatter by now as they too felt the agony in their backs.

The morning passed quickly if painfully, and the call for a dinner break was appreciated by all. Everyone gathered at a sheltered spot on the edge of the field and they were handed food and drinks by Hilde and Frau Muller.

The hour break was over far too quickly. They stretched their aching backs and resumed their work all over again as the spinner went into action. They all welcomed the setting sun; it meant it was time to go home. Tired and weary they sat on the wagon just comforting each other, knowing very well how each one felt.

Marta often marvelled at the farmers' capacity to cope with problems; quite often an animal was ill or having difficulties producing an offspring. Farmers often had to sit up during the night in damp places to give a helping hand if needed. The hours were long and irregular, especially at harvest time. In Mata's opinion farmers toiled far more than most people. However hard a farmer may appear, he will not ignore a suffering beast.

The time she had spent at Marien Hof made an everlasting impression upon her, and she realised even then that this was the environment she felt happiest in. She felt so contented and fulfilled living in the countryside and working with animals.

Sadly, all good things come to an end. Marta was suddenly called home because her mother was ill and so she was needed back in Hamburg. Arrangements were made for her departure.

She went across to see Hanne to say goodbye. Hanne was very upset at the news.

'See you when you return,' were her parting words.

At Marien Hof they all seemed genuinely sad at her leaving. Even Frau Muller, the frail looking figure who never showed any signs of emotion. She asked Marta to come into her private room and gave her advice for the future. She was a very religious woman Marta gathered by displayed pictures and figures of Jesus. They had no children of their own.

'Be good and go straight in life,' she told Marta. She even went so far as to say, 'You have been a good and honest working girl and it has been a pleasure having you here.'

Then Frau Muller gave Marta some money and with her blessing said goodbye.

Farewell Marien Hof

AS MARTA WENT THROUGH THE HOUSE AND OUT OF THE door for the last time she was greeted with joy by Lord, the Alsatian. What a terrible thing to do to say goodbye to this creature she had come to love so much.

'Oh, Lord,' she cried, putting her arms around his neck, the tears rolling down into his fur. He licked her face as he had done many times before, whimpering because he did not understand why his beloved friend was not her usual happy self.

'I shall miss you so,' she whispered into his ear. Her sorrow knew no bounds at this parting.

At that moment a gentle hand lifted her away from the dog. 'It's time to go,' Karl said quietly, 'or you'll be late for the train.'

She nodded and followed him to the waiting cart, with Polly in harness. Waving her last goodbye to Hilde, Herr and Frau Muller she could not help seeing as she glanced back that they too were wiping tears from their faces. It gave her a warm feeling inside to think that they liked her as much as that.

Marta and Karl sat in silence for a while as they trotted briskly down the lane, but she could sense that Karl kept looking at her. He realised that Marta was a desirable young woman now, and that she was going away. Then, in a clumsy sort of way, he told her he was very fond of her.

Marta was pleased to see the small railway station ahead, not sure what to say to him about this.

'Will you write to me?' he pleaded.

'Yes, I will do that,' she answered, thinking to herself that although she felt nothing more than friendship for this kind young man she did not want to hurt him. The pleased look on his face was her reward.

She felt she could not handle any more emotional upset, and was thankful to see the train puffing into the station.

Helping her off the cart he squeezed her hand, then lifted up her case and followed her to the train. 'Here is a seat by the window,' he pointed out to her.

Marta hastened in opening the door and Karl handed the case to her. After he had closed the door she pulled the window down to say her last goodbye. As the train slowly pulled away she waved until his forlorn figure was out of sight.

Exhausted by all the emotional upheaval of the day, she sank back into her seat. Her heart was aching as if it would break. With a dull, resigned look she watched as the countryside was left behind and more built-up areas began to appear. As the skyline of Hamburg came into view she thought, *I am going home. What is it going to be like to have buildings, noise and fumes surrounding me again after the wide-open space I have just left behind me?*

Marta stepped off the train into the hustle and bustle of the big city. She shuddered: traffic and people hurrying everywhere, but within seconds, however, she became one of them again, looking for a tram to take her home. She walked briskly to the flat, wondering what she was going to find.

The lodger (as she always referred to him) opened the door and she could hear Mutti calling her name. Forgetting all she had left behind, she fell on her knees by the bedside. Mutti looked so old and ill, but she was overjoyed to have her daughter back with her. Marta could feel the tears welling up in her eyes at the sight of her mother in this sorry state.

After they had talked for a while Marta realised she felt hungry. Going into the kitchen she found there was little food to be had. Fortunately Hilde had put some bread, wurst, cheese and cake into her bag, so she was able to offer her mother a good country-style meal, the sort that she herself had become used to eating at Marien Hof. Mutti was so pleased to see Marta so healthy and strong, with her golden tan, looking so attractive. She was so proud of her.

Meet the Other Half

UNFORTUNATELY FOR MARTA HER MOTHER DID NOT improve in health, and once more fate decreed that her life was to suffer another upheaval. Mutti was taken into hospital and the authorities were concerned about Marta's welfare. At seventeen she was under age and staying at the flat with the lodger was not considered to be morally right for her, so the question arose; who was next of kin? Her father, of course. So without further delay he was contacted to take care of his youngest daughter.

Once more, case in her hand, she was to travel to Leipzig. During the journey she wondered what her life was going to be like with this other half of her family she had heard so little of ever since Heinrich had been taken away by his father all those years ago.

Her mind was in turmoil by the time the train drew into Leipzig station. Slowly she got off the train and immediately saw her father waiting for her, his tall figure, with the mass of prematurely white hair, stood out in the crowd. He was scanning the faces of passengers as they alighted onto the platform. He recognised Marta immediately and rushed towards her.

As he folded her in his arms and hugged her to him nothing stirred inside her at all. She was devoid of feelings for this man who had, until this moment, ignored her existence. Did he really think that all the misery he had caused Mutti, Hans and herself could just be wiped out as if it had never happened?

'You are the image of your mother,' he said to Marta, as he took her case and guided her out of the station.

On the way to his flat he talked non-stop about his life in Leipzig. The flat was pleasant and well-furnished, very clean and tidy, not a bit like the flat in Hamburg.

Heinrich was not at home, but her sister Klara was there to welcome her. *How beautiful she is*, thought Marta. She had long, shining blonde hair, deep blue eyes and her movements were very graceful, not so boisterous compared to Father.

As she greeted the sister she hardly knew, Marta could sense that there was no bond of affection between them. She felt out of place and ill at ease. What would she feel like when she met Heinrich again? He was missed so much when her father had taken him away from Hamburg. She did not have to wait long to find out; he walked into the flat with fast movements, similar to father. He was tall and well-built with blond wavy hair and cool blue eyes. He was in every sense his father's son.

His greeting of, 'Hallo, Marta,' was as casual as if he had seen her only yesterday. She felt an overwhelming sense of disappointment, because he was the one she hoped to find support in, but his main concern seemed to be what they were going to have for dinner.

After speaking to Father he went to his room, singing various arias from various operas until the meal was served.

Her father worked as a print setter n the daytime but acted on stage at the Opera House every night. This meant that he earned quite a lot of money. Klara was well educated and had a good job as a secretary. Heinrich was still at high school, receiving a very good education paid for privately by Father.

Marta thought of Hans and herself. What a different life they had known! She remembered Mutti's struggle to provide for them and she felt a feeling of revulsion towards her father.

Marta spent a lot of time on her own in the following weeks, but when ever she had a chance Klara would keep her company and helped her in many ways as they got to know each other. She gave Marta some of her dresses of good quality and also took her to a hairdresser to have her lovely light red hair shaped. It was after that that Marta realised that although she had not the classic beauty of her sister, she was no longer an ugly duckling. Her hair hung in curls to her shoulders, accentuating her lovely green eyes.

Oh, My Papa

HER FATHER ALWAYS STOOD OUT IN THE CROWD; HE WAS tall, a strong build with steel grey eyes looking at you with sharp intensity from under his bushy eyebrows, matched by a full head of white hair. Some people would call him handsome, which, of course, he was, and maybe that was the reason Marta's parents' marriage broke up.

He lived a double life; at his work as a print setter during the daytime, but after a hasty meal at home he soon set out again, walking to his beloved theatre to enter into the world of performers and the very serious business of opera.

Oh, the glamour and prestige to mingle with the famous!

He had all the ingredients and stature to present any character in great style, and he loved every minute of it. The world outside did not exist as they all prepared for action and to step on stage, transforming and presenting to the audience a fantasy of strange characters and tales.

It was not surprising that the people loved the theatre; for three hours they could forget sorrow and other unpleasant things, sitting in comfortable seats on plush red velvet, and as the lights slowly dimmed the curtains parted to expose the scenery of the advertised opera, taking you to the exotic locations of 'Madam Butterfly' or 'Aida', to mention only a few.

But for Marta all this was new – she had never experienced opera before – so when Father suggested she come with him to the theatre she had no idea what it was all about or what to expect.

He took her into the theatre, passing the attendant with a nod towards Marta. 'My daughter,' he said, passing without payment for a seat. With instruction to wait for him after the end, he pointed to a seat and left.

Not long after the lights went down and the music started. The place went silent as the curtain parted to a scene of 'Tosca'. Marta was watching the whole show with great awe. Opera is a heavy experience for a teenager who has never explored this kind of music.

Afterwards her father came rushing up to her as she waited in the doorway. Sweat pearls lingered on his forehead, his face still flushed from his performance. All the way walking home he talked excitingly about the show.

'Did you find me?' he asked Marta. 'What costume was I wearing?' he enquired.

Marta could tell this was all so very important to his heart.

He chuckled when she had to confess she was not so sure which character he had portrayed in which scene.

It was late when they finally got back to the flat and Marta felt tired after the long walk. Father was used to it but she bid him goodnight and was soon asleep.

Two days later, Marta's father asked her again to the theatre to see 'Tourandot'.

'You will like it,' he promised her. He even told her the story so that she would understand better. 'It's very colourful,' he emphasised, talking about a Chinese princess.

Well, as a matter of fact Marta *did* enjoy this opera very much, even the music was getting into her system, but best of all she recognised her father as the executioner when he stood there, bare-chested, his torso shining with grease, his face in fiendish make-up as he sharpened his sword, to chop the head off an unfortunate victim.

Father was very pleased to hear that his daughter enjoyed the music, so he informed her about the composer.

So followed a lot of evenings at the theatre, but in the end Marta found them too sad and always cried her little heart out.

One day Father had this notion: 'You can take a photo of me, on stage all alone tonight.'

'All right,' Marta agreed, as he was well-known as a master photographer with a very expensive camera, taking photos of all the performers. A big cupboard in the kitchen was full with negatives.

Arriving at the theatre he did not take Marta into the theatre, instead they walked up some stairs. Father entered a small room and explained to a man sitting there that he would like his daughter to take a photo of him in the second act.

'Okay, Paul,' the man nodded in agreement. 'We'll see to that.'
Father went away in a hurry.

The man smiled at Marta and told her to sit on a little stool. The place was actually the spotlight compartment, right at the top of the theatre. In cramped position Marta watched the first part of 'Fledermans'.

'Get the camera ready,' the man warned Marta as she tried to focus in an exciting state on the figure all alone on stage. Suddenly she felt a hand on her neck pulling her backwards. The man's voice sounded in her ears, 'Keep back, for God's sake.'

Confused, Marta tried to pick herself up in this cramped place. The man was busy with his spotlight. Marta stared down. Father was nowhere to be seen. She felt like crying; Father would be annoyed.

After the act was over it was the interval, and all the lights came on. Then the man apologised for his rough handling of her. He explained to her what had happened. As Marta had tried to focus she had moved her body forward to the opening, which meant that she could have fallen out into the audience, so he actually saved her from a near fatal accident. There was no photo of Father, of course, but he understood the crisis.

From now on their relationship was a bit more understanding, and Marta had a great respect for him. At home he was a hard man and no one would have dared cross him. He was a hard-working man, never smoked a cigarette or drank alcohol. Sunday was his day of rest, which was celebrated with a special meal and wine, after which he was pleased with himself and in jovial spirits. The rest of the evening was spent on games. Klara had an ivory set of Majong, and this was enjoyed by all, and many hours passed in tense rivalry. Mostly the spirit was happy in the flat, the challenge was exciting, but woe betide the loser...

Christmas was spent quietly, with Klara making the Christmas decoration for the table. Father was baking the traditional *Stollee*: he was very handy at cooking and baking having lived on his own for a long time after the divorce.

The most remarkable coincidence in the family history after the split in the partnership was that never at any time had the four children met all together.

Meeting her father was very educational for Marta. He tried to give her a foundation by sending her to a private school to learn shorthand and typing. Yes, Marta had to admit; she discovered a lot about him, his way of thinking, his reasons for leaving Mutti and how to live. After all is said and done, she was his daughter and so inherited some of his characteristics too. Actually, she found out that in spite of resembling her mother to a tee, inside her there was Father's way of looking at life.

Her father began to take this attractive daughter to the theatre with him and show her off to his colleague behind the scene. He played a game asking her to see if she could recognise him on stage in his various disguises.

On their way home he talked of nothing but opera, his very own world, and Marta was not impressed or interested. She did enjoy 'Madam Butterfly', 'La Boheme' and 'Turandot', but to her mind they were all so sad.

Then one day Father told Marta to get dressed and he took her to a private school to learn shorthand and typing. *Now this is not too bad*, she thought, at least she was not in the flat all day getting bored. She needed cheering up.

Life was bad enough with all the news surrounding Hitler and his uprising. The threat of war, instead of peace hung like a dark cloud over everyone.

Klara decided to get married to a longstanding friend, Eric. He was very nice but Marta felt that they were not a well-matched couple.

Father also had a woman friend of longstanding coming to the flat, she was not a beauty, but of genuine good nature. Klara and her new husband moved into a flat of their own.

Whatever made Klara decide to get married was unknown, but one rainy day they gathered together for this occasion, celebrating at home in style, blissfully unaware of the dark, evil clouds gathering momentum between life and death…

A Blanket on the Ground

THE DAY WAR WAS DECLARED REMAINED FOR EVER IN MARTA'S memory. Heinrich had just come home very downcast and worried because he had to tell his father the news that he had failed an examination. He lay on the sofa listening to the radio, trying to take his mind off his problem. At that moment came the announcement that Germany was at war.

'Oh well,' Heinrich commended philosophically, 'that will save me telling Father, I shall be called up now, it can wait.'

Sure enough, within three days he received his marching orders. *He's taking it rather nonchalantly*, Marta thought. Klara's husband quickly followed him, so she came back to the flat to be with Marta for company again. They often went out together.

One day they were looking in some shops when Klara spotted an old acquaintance; a tall, handsome fellow, who to Marta seemed more suited to her sister than her husband was. They greeted each other excitedly and started exchanging news.

'Let's go to a beer garden,' he suggested.

When they arrived there the conversation was animated between the two of them. Marta was bored and she passed the time playing with a passing cat which came up to her.

They were still talking as he accompanied them home, while Marta pondered, *Why did Klara not marry this one?*

They made such a striking couple. He was devastatingly handsome, with his black hair and dark eyes; a perfect foil for Klara's blonde beauty.

Her fantasy was interrupted by her sister telling her to say goodbye to him.

As they walked upstairs Marta asked, 'Is he married?' Klara shook her head. 'How old is he?' was the next question.

'About twenty-five,' was the reply.

'Why didn't you marry him?' Marta asked and then stopped, because she could see that something was troubling Klara.

The next evening Klara and Marta were doing some sewing. They were alone together in the flat; their father had gone to the Opera House as usual. The doorbell rang and Klara asked Marta to see who it was.

'It's the downstairs bell,' she called as Marta left the room.

Closing the flat door behind her, Marta ran down the flight of stairs in her youthful way. As she opened the outside door she saw there at the roadside stood the handsome fellow from the night before. By his side was a gleaming motorbike.

'Hallo,' he greeted Marta. 'Will you come for a ride with me?' he asked.

Marta thought, *He can't mean me, surely he means Klara.*

However, it was her he was asking.

'Well, I'd better ask Klara first,' she stammered at this unusual proposal.

She raced back up the stairs and into the flat. Klara lifted her hear as Marta blurted out, 'It's that fellow we met last night, and he has asked me to go for a ride with him on his motorbike.' She watched Klara's face for the affect this would have on her.

'Hell, you had better get dressed and go,' her sister said, surprisingly unruffled. 'He must have noticed how pretty you are.'

Hurriedly Marta dressed herself in trousers, jumper and jacket and then went downstairs with mixed feelings about it all.

The night before Klara had been aglow meeting this man again, but she was married. Why should she mind him asking Marta out?

Reaching the outside door her thoughts of Klara vanished as he came smiling over to her. He escorted her to the motorbike, and after putting his cap and goggles on he told Marta to get on the pillion and seat herself closely behind him. He instructed her to keep a tight hold of him as he sped out of Leipzig.

Marta had never been on a motorbike before, and was quite scared, especially going round corners. Eventually he slowed down at a forest a few miles out of the city. He entered a small clearing and stopped the engine. They both got off and after he made sure his bike stood safely he pulled out a blanket from a box behind the seat and spread it on the ground.

Marta watched this with apprehensive feelings and all kinds of thoughts were racing through her head. Was this to be her first encounter of the 'unknown'? Sex and relations with a man... Oh, yes! She had to admit he was the right type for her imagination...

He invited her to sit on the blanket and then, taking off his jacket, he sat down beside her. Marta sat tense and rigid, wondering what would happen next. He talked, asking questions about herself and then said he liked what he saw. She dared not say too much, seeing his dark eyes like a deep pool of no return so close to her face. A shiver ran through her body. It was getting dark and chilly, so she asked him to take her home. She wanted to be back before her father returned from the theatre. He was very strict and liked to know her whereabouts.

Politely he helped Marta up, put the blanket away and quickly got the motorbike ready for the road. In a short time they were back in Leipzig. He stopped outside the flats, and as Marta got off the pillion and walked to the door he followed her.

Suddenly and without warning she found herself in his arms and being kissed in a manner she had never experienced before. It was a burning kiss of desire. She pulled away from him and hastily opened the door, saying goodnight and promising to see him again.

Marta leaned against the inside of the door as she listened to the sound of the motorbike fading away in the distance.

'Oh my God!' she muttered to herself as her blood seemed to race through her body.

Slowly, she climbed the stairs to the flat, trying to gain her confidence before facing Klara. Her face was burning and her heart was beating very irregularly. She had to calm her emotions before entering the flat.

Trying to appear casual she went straight into the kitchen to pour herself a cool drink. Sipping from the glass she walked into the other room to face Klara.

'Did you enjoy your trip?' she asked, looking up and smiling.

'Yes, very much,' Mara replied, but before Klara could ask any more questions Marta yawned. 'The fresh air has made me feel tired. I think I will go to bed,' and she moved into the bedroom.

In the privacy and darkness of her bedroom Marta relaxed and recalled Helmut's dark, smouldering eyes as he gazed at her and felt his burning lips on hers. Could this be her first encounter with love, she wondered? When they had sat in the clearing in the forest he could so easily have forced himself upon her; she wouldn't have stood a chance if he had done so. Instead he had behaved like a gentleman and not taken advantage of her. Chivalry was sill a virtue in those days. Wondering what the future might hold for them, Marta dropped off to sleep with a happy smile on her lips.

Fate decided to intervene once more in her life…

The following lunchtime the doorbell downstairs rang and taking the steps two at a time Marta flew down to see who was there. Her heart lurched as she saw that it was indeed the man of her dreams standing there. Instead of greeting her happily he held her hands in his own and explained sadly that he had come to say goodbye. His motorbike was to be confiscated that day and he had also received his call-up papers. Marta was so stunned by the news that she could not speak and tears welled up in her eyes. He squeezed her hands tightly and then, releasing them quickly, returned to his motorbike, and lifting his hand in a farewell salute was gone from her life as quickly as he had entered it. He was never to know the impact his kiss had made on a very innocent girl called Marta.

The shock suffered by this turn of events lingered on. Her heart was heavy as she walked slowly back into the flat. How happy she had been only minutes before as she had run down to open the door! The first bitter taste of war was affecting her.

In such a short time three young men near and dear to her had been called away to defend their Fatherland. After Marta had told Klara the news they both sat there in silence, each with their own thoughts.

Shortly after this a letter arrived saying Mutti was home again and Marta could return to Hamburg. Her father wanted her to stay in Leipzig, but she was eager to travel home as quickly as possible.

Sadly he realised that the love and care he had lavished on Marta in the past month had come too late. He held no place in her heart.

Now it was time for Marta to move on, back home to Mutti where she belonged and no one could stop her. Father lamented but was ignored; she was ready to move on, and he had no place in her heart.

Packing her few belongings didn't take long, and she was soon on her way to the station with Father in attendance; she was glad to get away as the train moved slowly out into the open.

As the train sped towards Hamburg Marta felt relieved that she was returning to Mutti and the place that had been her home during her childhood and formative years. She would rather share her mother's problems and put up with the untidiness of the flat than live in the so different world of her father.

Mutti's love was so warm, and the way that she expected so little from life was already implanted in Marta's soul; this bond could not be broken.

Her mother's joy at seeing her again touched her deeply. She realised that her mother had wondered if Marta would return after living such a different life with no shortage of anything in Leipzig.

'You look so grown up,' she said admiringly.

Return to Hamburg

'WELL, WELL, WE ARE MOVING UP IN THE WORLD,' MARTA commented to Mutti. 'Even your own art collection now!' She pointed to three pictures hanging on one wall. There were two pictures of country scenes sketched in charcoal. These were done by Klara. But dominating the wall was a big picture of an architectural design in black ink, preformed by Heinrich.

'Well, Mutti, haven't you got some talented children? It must be rubbing off Uncle Heini.'

Another picture was hanging between the two windows. It showed the head of a sleeping child, drawn in plain pencil form, but not lacking skill. It was done by Hans while he was home on leave.

Each picture presented a different style as observed by the painter, but the master of the family circle was of course Uncle Heini. One of his greatest paintings to Marta's mind was hanging in her room: a huge picture of Grandmother, sitting there in full posture, dressed in a long, drab skirt and a fitted bodice buttoned up to the neck. An apron completed this Victorian outfit. Her hands rested on her apron. Her grey hair was neatly parted in the middle and set in a bun at the back. Most impressive were here eyes, looking down at the viewer, following their moves in real life-like fashion, a cool grey and rather stern looking pair of eyes.

Life had taken on a new meaning for Marta, and she felt important as she walked through the rooms of the flat, which had been improved by the addition of paintings on the walls, all created by the members of the family, showing the potential inherited talent. But the most unusual factor was that it presented the whole of the family together.

As Heinrich was studying architecture he had presented his mother with a huge picture of an impressive building done in black ink which dominated the wall. In contrast, on each side were the country scenes sketched in charcoal by Klara. What a lovely gesture and tribute to their mother who they knew so little about!

Not to be left out of the gathering of paintings, Marta too had given Mutti one of her favourite subject; a painted horse's head. It was hanging behind a door; Mutti had no love for horses and did not share her daughter's passion.

At that stage the future ahead seemed promising with Hans doing so well at his newfound profession.

The whole family was beginning to get together more often, but that was not meant to be – destiny decided otherwise…

Moral Conflicts

MARTA WAS VERY PLEASED TO LEARN THAT HANNE HAD returned to Hamburg after her time was up at the farm and she lost no tine in getting in touch with her. They arranged to meet the following Saturday to go to a small dance hall nearby, hoping for a bit of fun and relaxation.

Sitting at a small table sipping apple juice they waited to be asked to dance; while they were not overwhelmed by offers, they were not exactly wallflowers. One good dance was all Marta needed and she was in heaven. If they didn't like the partner of the evening they would sneak out, laughing as they parted to go home.

On other occasions the offer to escort them home was accepted, but as far as Marta was concerned this always ended up in a distressing battle. Letting herself be kissed held some attraction, but when hands became exploratory over her body something snapped inside her. She was not ready for sex – especially not in a doorway or just for the fun of it with a guy she hardly knew. Often she lay in her bed confused after her feelings. In all her innocence she believed that sex outside marriage was not possible for her to do. Then again, the subject of marriage was a very touchy one after her parents' fiasco. She would have to be very sure if she did get married, remembering the tragic impact of her family splitting up and the effect it had on her life and Mutti's in particular.

The unknown future often frightened her as womanhood approached. For all her experience in life she was still very naïve for her age. At this time life became more stable for a while when Marta found a good job at a large factory making medical supplies. It was clean work and regular pay.

She was able to buy a brand new bicycle to travel to and from work. Mutti was happy too because Marta was able to pay for her keep and help with the rent. Her room was improved with new curtains and a bedspread, making it pleasant to be in. Life seemed to be on the up and up at last.

Easter time brought the promise of spring, so Marta decided to treat herself to a new outfit: a white skirt, pale blue blouse and flowered jacket. Admiring herself in the mirror, she thought, *I wonder if Hanne will like this*, as she happily went on her way to meet her.

'You are late,' her friend said, eyeing her new outfit appraisingly. 'Very nice, it suits you,' she commented, 'but come on, let's get going.' Her face was full of anticipation as they hurried along to the usual dance hall.

It was their great pleasure in life, and didn't cost them much for an evening of sheer enjoyment. While the opposite sex seemed to need to drink before they enjoyed dancing, all the girls needed was the music to dance.

The evening passed quickly, the last dance was over and soon they were on their way home, unaccompanied this time.

'Goodnight, see you tomorrow,' Hanne said as they parted.

Marta decided to take a shortcut across a piece of wasteland. If only she had taken her usual route home it would have saved her from a very distressing incident.

She was totally unaware of the danger that was awaiting her. Looking down as she picked her way through the overgrown grass she didn't notice that she was being followed. Suddenly she was grabbed from behind and thrown to the ground.

'Oh my God!' she cried. 'My new outfit will be ruined!'

It didn't seem to occur to her that it was her body that would be spoiled if the attacker had his way. The thought that Mutti would be angry with her for ruining her new clothes was utmost in her mind as she fought like a wildcat to get away. They rolled and struggled on the ground with Marta scratching, kicking and fighting with every ounce of strength she could muster. Her assailant must have been surprised by the fierce struggle she put up, because after what seemed an eternity she broke away from his grasp. Running and stumbling she managed to reach the road. She dared not look around to see if she was being followed, she just kept on running the rest of the way home.

She was thankful that no one was around when she arrived at

the flat. Creeping up to her bedroom she collapsed exhausted and shaking onto her bed. She cried bitterly when she saw how dirty her lovely new clothes were, but at least a washing would put matters right again.

As she started to undress ready to go to bed, the full implication of the attack hit her. She then realised how lucky she was to get away without being raped. She shuddered as she thought of the consequences this could have had. What did clothes matter when she had managed to escape such a fate? Counting her blessings she was grateful that she had been given such strength at that fearful time. She sobbed bitterly until finally sleep overcame her and her aching body was able to relax.

Never did Marta mention the episode to anyone, not even Hanne. She thought no one would believe her. Rape and sex abuse were not headlines in those days. The fear of walking alone in dark and lonely places never left her.

Another lesson learnt the hard way…

Teenagers' Pleasures

ON A HAPPIER NOTE, MARTA AND HANNE DECIDED TO ATTEND their first fancy dress ball. They made their costumes in readiness and decided to wear *Dirnlkleid*, a national dress which consisted of a gathered, printed skirt, a white blouse with large puffed sleeves and a black velvet waistcoat.

The ball was held in a large dance hall, and anyone under twenty-one years of age could not attend without an adult escort. Mutti was delighted to be their chaperon, remembering how much she herself enjoyed such occasions.

Excited, they travelled to the venue and could hear the music before entering. Hanne gasped as they went into the dance hall.

'Oh, Marta!' she breathed, 'isn't it exciting?' her face beaming with pleasure.

They found a table and waited hopefully to be asked to dance. They were a bit depressed when a little middle-aged fellow kept coming up to them and asking either Marta or Hanne for a dance until Mutti stepped in and told him to look for someone his own age. He got the message and didn't trouble them again. Good old Mutti!

Young men were scarce at the time, but Marta and Hanne danced the evening away together until the early hours of the morning. Mutti had already gone home and was tired after her hard-working days. The two friends walked home through the empty streets, shoes in their hands, cooling their hot and aching feet on the pavements. The dawn was breaking on the horizon as if heralding a new beginning. They laughed and giggled in their girlish way.

Having spent such a pleasant time dancing the night away, they didn't realise it was the end of an era. That happy evening belonged to a past which would soon be gone forever. Days would dawn, but with time a new image would rise and change all the old ways into a fast-moving, fast-growing time of a different mankind...

A Birthday Drama

Early in October Marta treated herself to a special birthday present; a portable gramophone and a few of her favourite records. She was so excited that she could not wait to tell a friend at work about it. They both belonged to a water sports club, going canoeing in groups at weekends on the canals and rivers which flowed through the surrounding countryside. Sometimes they took camping equipment and stayed out for the weekend.

'What about a camping weekend for your birthday?' Marta's workmate suggested.

'It's a bit late in the year for travelling in a canoe,' Marta said doubtfully.

'Oh, come on! I will get a few pals together. It will be fun,' was the reply.

Sure enough the other girl soon organised everything. Herself and her boyfriend, another couple and a boy with a canoe for Marta.

As the weekend approached Marta became quite excited about this little adventure arranged to celebrate her eighteenth birthday. Young and sometimes foolish, she decided to take her new gramophone and records so that they could all enjoy the music that evening. 'Man supposes – God disposes,' as the saying goes…

Marta was quite laden down by the time she arrived at the boathouse. The others were already there and the canoes were ready for the journey.

'Come on, slowcoach! Get your gear into the canoe,' someone called.

'We are ready for the off!'

The boys closed the doors of the boathouse while the girls got into the canoes.

Within minutes they were gliding through the water.

'Where are we going?' Marta asked the boy she was sharing the canoe with.

'No idea,' was the reply, 'it's up to Otto, the leader.'

They travelled along for quite some time and eventually came to a lock, and after it had filled up the big gates opened and they were heading out to the open water of the River Elbe. This was where big ships from foreign lands came to dock at the port of Hamburg.

What different elements faced the three canoes; the water was choppy, and a cool wind blew against them as they battled against a strong current. Marta's shoulders ached from the effort as they tried to keep fairly close to the others. *What foolish nonsense this is*, she thought.

Then the command came from Otto; 'To the left,' and thankfully they reached a calmer waterway.

'That's better,' Marta sighed with relief. The pace had slowed down and they were travelling close together within talking distance.

By now the daylight had gone but a large silver moon was shining on the water and lighting their way.

'We are looking for a camping site now,' Otto announced. 'Keep your eyes open.'

Marta looked around her. *He must be joking*, she thought, *or perhaps he is lost and is now hoping someone else will know where we are.*

Gliding through the water they scanned the darkness for a suitable place to land. Suddenly someone shouted, 'There you are, right in front of us. The ideal place.'

All eyes followed the direction of the pointing hand, and sure enough, there in the moonlight was a sandy beach. It was like a mirage to the weary travellers. They couldn't believe it existed until the canoes actually grounded on the sand.

The front person in each canoe jumped out and pulled it further out of the water and then they were dragged to a higher point securing them to some trees which were luckily growing there. Between them they soon emptied the canoes, and while the boys began to erect the two tents the girls made a drink for them all. The mood was more relaxed now they were on dry land again. The tents in order, cushions and blankets were put down and they sat together eating sandwiches and drinking tea. The boys called for some music.

Marta happily obliged by playing one of her records, but everyone was so tired that it wasn't really appreciated properly. The struggle through the choppy water and strong current had taken its toll, so instead of having a happy birthday party they all decided to go to sleep. Marta shared a tent with the other girls. As club members there was a code to be obeyed and the girls respected this.

Some hours later Marta awoke. She sensed something was wrong when she heard a gurgling sound. Carefully, so that she wouldn't wake the others, she crept and peered through the slit in the front of the tent. 'Oh no!' What a sight met her eyes; water, water everywhere, no sign of the sandy beach.

Her horrified gaze fell on her precious gramophone and records surrounded by water which was seeping into the tent as the tide was coming in. The adventure hadn't taken into account that they were on the banks of a tidal river!

'Everybody up!' she called, but no one took any notice.

Groans of 'Go to sleep!' greeted her.

She started shouting at them that the tide was coming in quickly and they were already surrounded by water. That made them spring into action.

Stepping out into the icy water, there was no room for being squeamish as the cold slipped into the body. They quickly emptied and dismantled the tents. Everything was put in the canoes and all they could do was huddle in them with a canvas over the boat until daylight.

To make matters worse it started to rain heavily so they decided to make for home when there was sufficient light. It was no fun being wet and cold lying in a canoe. Marta was dreading the hazardous journey through the open river again, and sure enough it was tough going. The canoes bounced on the choppy surface, sometimes drifting away from each other. Conditions worsened and panic began to set in.

Fortunately, a passing barge noticed their predicament and came close and shouted to throw a line. Marta was only too happy to oblige. There were difficulties balancing, but they succeeded in the end. What a relief when all their canoes were taken in tow and pulled to the safety of the lock and inland waterways!

So ended an unforgettable birthday for Marta as she made her way home, cold and miserable, not to mention the tiredness in her bones. Although her records were slightly spoiled, the gramophone dried out all right and provided a lot of pleasure to Marta.

A Party Invitation

A LETTER FROM HANS ARRIVED WITH AN INVITATION TO attend a party at a naval base near Hamburg. Could Marta rustle up a couple of females to go with her, he wanted to know?

'How about it? Are you coming, Hanne?' she asked her friend. Hanne had recently got engaged to Werner who she had met at the dance hall, but was now away in the army.

'Will there be any dancing?' she enquired. Dancing was more of a temptation to resist than the prospect of meeting a lot of young fellows.

'Kate has already agreed to come because she is fond of Hans,' Marta told her.

'Okay, I will come, but don't tell my mother about this,' Hanne said to her.

Marta understood. 'You are staying the weekend with me, okay?'

Marta wrote to Hans and told him that she had persuaded Hanne to come along with Kate and herself.

As arranged they travelled to Rerik and were met by Hans. 'You look great,' he commented, feeling quite proud to be able to present not one but three good-looking girls to his friends: black-haired, blue-eyed, shapely Hanne; Kate with a totally different kind of beauty – a mass of curly brown hair surrounded her doll-like face setting off her alluring green eyes; and Marta really had grown into a very attractive girl with her mass of red hair, Hans thought as he looked admiringly at his sister.

Hans told them to go into the hall while he changed his uniform, but they decided to wait outside for him instead. It was not long before he came striding back looking very smart indeed. He took his charges inside and introduced Marta and Hanne to two sergeants while he escorted Kate. Hanne was quite taken with her chosen partner, but what a choice Marta had! *Not at all my type*, she thought. He couldn't even dance. *I am in for a boring evening*, she thought despondently. Then, to her astonishment, a handsome young naval man came up to her, bowed and asked her if she was free to dance. Oh boy! She was free and ready.

He was a very good dancer, and as they moved around the dance floor he enquired about her escort. Marta explained the situation and he was so pleased that the sergeant meant nothing to her.

They eventually danced outside as the music drifted through the open windows and doors. *Just like you see in the movies*, Marta thought. Moonlight on the water, she in the arms of a handsome fellow... They kissed in the shadows and for a moment the world did not exist.

Then the romantic spell was broken by the appearance of Hans. 'There you are! It's time to go home,' he said, urging Marta away.

As she reluctantly said goodbye to her romantic partner, Hans whispered, 'Looking for higher status, were you?'

She didn't get his meaning. 'Why do you say that?' she asked him.

He nodded towards the naval chap. 'He is an officer, and by the look of him, probably married. Beware, sister,' he warned, 'the word is full of them.'

Despite his warning Marta stayed on cloud number nine for quite a while.

Hanne also looked happy with herself. Kate never did show any emotion, but there was no doubt she must have enjoyed herself being with Hans.

So it turned out to be an evening well spent away from the daily strain of work as the clouds of war spread menacingly overhead. Soon happiness was to cease and horror would take its place. These clouds had no silver linings...

Now life seemed all right. Marta was still working in the factory making medical supplies for the fighting men. It was hard work, but it was pleasant getting to know new people –mostly young ones like herself.

One day Erica asked Marta if she like to go with her to a dance club. 'Yes, that would be lovely!' Marta said, so a meeting place was arranged for later.

Happily Marta went on her way, and together they stepped into a hall. Erica was greeted by two fellows and she introduced Marta to the chaps and the taller one offered himself as her partner. His name was Karl and he was quite to her liking, so they met again. Romance soon blossomed and he proposed marriage because Marta was not a girl to have sex before marriage. She agreed, so soon a date was fixed.

November: a dull day. Even Hans, her brother, came for the ceremony. All went well without wedding bells or blessing; a war was on – a depressing thought, but Marta was young and excited and they got a little flat, and nothing clouded their harmony.

Father provided news that Heinrich was to go and fight with the Desert Rats under Rommel's Pancercorp, and Eric, Klara's husband, was missing. The first casualty was a shock to the system. Klara was dead!

Father summoned Marta to Leipzig, and as a well-behaved daughter she went with mixed feelings, but Hans got leave and was also there to bring comfort to his young sister to cope with this tragedy.

Klara, this beautiful woman had killed herself! Why?

Father had no explanation that made any sense So desperate to take her own life…

Back home there was more horror on the horizon of destruction. Never before in the history of killings had the human race inflicted such savage fury on innocent people, whatever the race or belief.

Marta was not a patriot or bias to any such cause. No person of sound mind would have planned such a turbulent lifestyle, putting life in jeopardy to test courage.

Turning Point

NOW THE WAR WAS SHOWING SIGNS OF ENDING AS THE famous Paneer Corp under the command of Field Marshall Rommel (the Desert Fox, as he was called), were defeated and had to retreat from their base in North Africa. The battle of El Alamein was over. Heinrich was serving there as a lance corporal, but no news was received from him.

Hans, meanwhile, was at the Russian front. He had served there for some time as an anti-aircraft gunner. They had fought their way as far as Stalingrad but were now in retreat. The conditions were atrocious and there was much suffering. The news from him was calm without alarm on his part. He had everything planned, saving his pay in a bank account. Once the war was over he was going to make sure he could afford a house for him and Kate with enough space for Mutti and Marta. In his will the money was left to Marta to take care of Mutti for the rest of her life.

His dream was never to be realised. Destiny intended otherwise. Their lives were to be changed beyond the wildest realms of imagination...

On the home front life was becoming a nightmare. It was all work, queuing for rations of food and hours spent in air raid shelters.

Almost every night the sirens roused them from their sleep and they would hastily fling clothes on and with a few precious belongings flee to the nearest shelter or bunker. There they would stay as the bombers flew over Hamburg on their way to Berlin.

This was not a healthy existence. There was little relaxation as all places of entertainment including dance halls were closed. The one thing enjoyed by Marta and Hanne was the music from the records they collected. Whenever they had a chance they would spend time in Marta's room playing the dance music on a new record player, a polished cabinet with space for the records – Marta's pride and joy. Often Hanne would stay for the weekend and they would lie in bed listening to the records or radio.

'A Little on the Lonely Side' was a very appropriate song.

Marta was very fond of buying American records, especially the big band sound, she particularly enjoyed playing these.

A Foolish Hero

THE WAR WAS ON THE BRINK OF COLLAPSE AS HANS unexpectedly appeared on the scene, finding them through the system of registration. After the retreat from Russia he had been posted to Northern Italy. He was a sergeant major now. Travelling with him was a corporal and a private. He had decided to make a detour to see if Mutti and Marta were all right. What a shock he had when he saw their miserable existence! He had been through some horrific experiences on the Russian Front, which had hardened him, but the sight of his mother, sister and Kate with her daughter living in this degrading manner upset him a great deal.

One thing Marta never quite understood was that despite the retreat from Russia and other fronts Hans still believed in a miracle. *Who is he kidding, himself?* she thought. *Is he a fool or a true soldier obeying orders?* She would never really know...

Late one afternoon Hans, Kate and the private went out to look at the old places, now unrecognisable. Mutti had gone out to work. The corporal stayed with Marta, and as they talked together she found out that he came from Switzerland but was of German origin and had been called up.

He watched Marta intently with his smouldering dark eyes. He moved closer to her and kissed her, then suggested going to bed with her.

She was furious, 'What a darn cheek!' she reproachfully exclaimed. That was the last thing she wanted on her troubled mind. Firmly she put him in his place, but instead of him losing interest she had gained his respect. He apologised to her for losing control over his emotions. He explained that being a soldier in the thick of the fighting he had been deprived of all pleasures for a long time. Here he was with an attractive girl in his arms, warm and tempting. Could she blame him for wanting her? Marta understood his point (not to the full extent), but did not allow him any liberties.

They talked of many things after that, and time passed quickly. The others returned and soon it was time for the men to leave. Marta and Kate went with them to the station. The corporal asked Marta to write to him and she promised to do so. She liked the man, for all that he had hoped to seduce her after so short an acquaintance. He told her she had gained his respect and he could trust her completely. A last kiss for him and her brother and the train moved out of the station. It was the last goodbye...

Marta did receive two letters from him, full of love for her. He was separated from Hans, then silence. Three months later a letter arrived for her, from a stranger with news that her corporal had been killed in action. The writer was his brother and he had heard all about her. Even his parents in Switzerland knew about her. The brother asked if she would write to him, but she decided that this chapter was closed as far as she was concerned. She was in no mood for romance.

After all her experiences and failures to find someone to love, to cherish, for better for worse, in sickness and in health, till death do us part – a foolish thought!

Where have all the young men gone? To a war, everyone.

Her youth was lost with the passing of time.

The years went by in a very turbulent fashion, disturbing to the mind. Just getting married was one thing, but when Hans started asking questions about Karl not getting called up what with him looking a healthy young man...

It started Marta thinking: he disappeared over periods of time, claiming he was working elsewhere. She trusted him, but what was his secret?

Then it dawned on her: his family were Jewish but he had a different name. His mother married someone who adopted Karl under his name, but as the war was raging on the mystery was not solved.

In 1945 when the war was at an end, Marta sued for divorce, which was granted without opposition. Four years had passed in between. She was young no more, and had endured nothing worth recalling.

She wanted a dream marriage, like her uncle Heini and Julia

had, but the future was meaningless, crippled and isolated. There was no end to it, no future…

Nothing was heard about Hans's fate till Mutti received a parcel from the Red Cross. It contained a wallet and the identity disc belonging to Hans. He had been killed in action – just five days before the war ended, shot in the back by partisans in northern Italy.

A letter explaining it was written by a lieutenant who was leading the party at the time and was taken prisoner. That was why it had taken so long to report. The irony? His savings for Mutti and Kate were in a bank that became the Russian part of Germany, and no one got the benefit as intended. Kate never married again and lived quietly with her daughter.

Fire Duties

THE NIGHT ATTACKS BECAME MORE FREQUENT AND HAMBURG was one of the prime targets. The air raid sirens became a familiar and dreaded sound, soon followed by the menacing and threatening sound of humming aeroplanes moving overhead to drop their deadly charges.

There was no escape from the sound of bombs raining down from the sky and the noise after the explosion. The sight of fires raging all over the city and the acrid smell which followed was something never to be forgotten by all the unfortunate, helpless people who experienced intense bombing raids, the not knowing if your relatives and friends were among the victims, the horror on people's faces when they returned from shelters to find their homes destroyed.

Marta was among the girls who had to stay behind after work to be trained for firefighting in the factories. Sometimes they were on night duty at the place they worked and other times they were sent to a large industrial complex on the outskirts of the city. The girls hated this. Watching in strange, dark factories and dreading the wail of the sirens, they felt so vulnerable as the bombs began their swift and deadly destruction.

On the nights that she was not on duty Marta would have loved an uninterrupted night's sleep; working all day and then having to endure long hours of air raids she became exhausted. *How do we stay sane?* she often wondered. They say disaster brings out the best in people and this is very true, but why do human beings destroy one another in this way? If there is a God why doesn't He prevent such misery? Looking back, a lot of people wondered how they survived those years of horror and hardship.

By now all the people who lived in the block of flats had moved their treasured possessions into the cellars, and Marta was no exception. Downstairs went her radio, her record player, the records neatly packed in a strong box, a basket full of clothes and her bicycle.

One night the sirens wailed and as she made her way to the shelter Marta looked up at the clear, star-studded night and in the beam of a searchlight she saw an enemy aircraft. It was an eerie feeling to think that she was at the mercy of the enemy in that bomber. The thought in her mind was, *Will there be another dawn to see?*

There was…

The Red Omen

THE WEATHER WAS HOT, MAKING WORK AN EVEN MORE TIRING task. Marta planned to go swimming after work in the outdoor swimming pool. *That will soothe my aching body*, she declared to herself. No such luck, however.

Her name was on the duty sheet for firefighting at the industrial complex at Hamburg. 'Oh no! Not that dreaded place again,' she wailed.

Then she thought of Hans and Heinrich in the thick of fighting and sighed. There was a war on and she had been trained to fight firebombs in factories, so she must just get on with it. How stupid this killing, the whole war. When would it all end? Striding down to the S Bahn station she could hear a train approaching and started to hurry up the stairs over the platform. She boarded the train just in the nick of time. The other girls were waiting at their meeting place to take another train to Hamburg.

After exchanging views of what they would have rather done on such a beautiful hot summer's night, they set off for their destination.

Near to the factory they were going to was an anti-aircraft post. The soldiers on duty whistled at the girls and beckoned them to come over.

'No,' Marta said, 'we can't do that.'

'You are a spoilsport,' the girls said as they shook their heads in the direction of the soldiers and instead made their way into the factory.

It felt chilly after the warmth outside. They walked up to the third floor where there was a storage area. The other girls settled down for a drink of Ersatz coffee while Marta went over to a large window and gazed at the panorama before her. The view was magnificent. The river Elbe was below and the port and city were outlined against the sky. She watched the sun setting over the river like a huge red fireball hanging in mid-air. As the translucent sun slowly disappeared it cast a glow over the surface of the water and the sky. It seemed like an omen to Marta as she stood transfixed by this spectacular sight caused by nature, unaware of the horror that lay in the wake of that red, red sunset.

As darkness approached a chill crept over her and she turned away from the window.

'Any coffee left?' she asked, and one of the girls handed her the remaining cupful.

'Thanks,' she said, sipping it thoughtfully.

Suddenly all hell broke loose.

The sirens sounding the alarm was nothing strange, but already they could hear the drone of approaching bombers. There seemed to be hundreds of them as they moved menacingly through the searchlights, and flak from the anti-aircraft guns headed steadily towards the city of Hamburg.

The girls watched in horror as the bombs started to fall not on the industrial complex but on the city itself. Marta felt as if her world was being destroyed before her eyes. It was like watching a movie, but this horror was for real. Crying hysterically the girls huddled together for comfort in the darkness. They had a grandstand view of the bombs hitting the targets, followed by explosions and fire. Where Marta had watched the red sunset the sky was now filled with smoke and fire.

'This must be hell,' she murmured.

They thought of their families and friends caught in the destruction and wondered what was happening to them.

It was over as suddenly as it had begun. The anti-aircraft guns ceased firing and the all clear sounded. 'To hell with this factory,' the girls agreed. 'Let's go home.' *If there is still a home to be found*, went through Marta's mind.

Pulling on their coats, bags over shoulders, they set off into the night for the journey back to Hamburg. There was no transport available, but that did not deter them.

The sky was alight with the raging fires and a pall of smoke hung over the city and the acrid smell of destruction was everywhere. The nearer they got to their destination the worse the chaos became. It was a sight which could never be described in a thousand words in any language. The sound of screaming people filled the air. There was panic all round and they became desperate to get to their own districts to find out what had happened.

Trying to pick their way over debris and avoid fires made progress tortuously slow. They felt as if they would never get nearer to their destination.

Eventually they parted to go their separate ways. By now a grey dawn was emerging from behind the dirty black clouds of smoke. As Marta struggled along she marvelled at the brave people who were tending the homeless and injured, heedless of falling debris and many explosions from fractured gas mains.

The firemen were desperately trying to put fires out, but were fighting a losing battle. People young and old were frantically moving rubble, calling the names of missing relatives and friends. The streets Marta knew so well could hardly be recognised.

Still a long way from home she decided to try and get away from the worst of the smoke and heat as she was feeling thirsty and sick.

A canal was not far away and she made her way in that direction. As she walked along the bank everything seemed unreal; the still murky water and all around a burning city.

Feeling so weary, when she saw a bench she decided to have a rest to gather strength for the rest of her journey. But the urgency of worry about Mutti moved her aching feet once more into action and eventually she ventured into the streets.

People were fleeing the city as loudspeakers were urging them on to leave. A whole district had been destroyed and the loss of this night ran into horrendous figures.

Struggling along between tramlines Marta finally reached home late afternoon. The block of flats stood intact, but the cul-de-sac was deserted. She went into the flat; everything seemed eerily quiet. The only person there was the lodger, who was in a drunken sleep. Relieved that the flat was undamaged but worried because Mutti was not there, she felt lost and wondered what to do next. She went into her room and lay on the bed.

'Oh, Mutti! What has happened to you? Where are you?' she whispered, exhausted. She fell asleep only to be awakened by the sirens wailing the alarm again.

Oh my God, not again! she thought as she staggered out of bed. She was still dressed so just pulled a coat on and ran for the shelter.

The next thing she remembered was the ground trembling like an earthquake, then darkness and oblivion claimed her.

Regaining consciousness, her eyes met something sticking out of her mouth as tubes were leading down to her stomach. A nurse bent over her. Gently she motioned to Marta to lie still. She was alive and in hospital. Tears rolled down her face. Was this really a blessing, feeling so lost and lonely?

As the night approached the hospital staff began to hurriedly move patients into a nearby bunker. All these activities went past her bed. They could not move Marta as she was too ill. She just lay staring vacantly into space, not caring if she lived or died.

Once more Hamburg was under attack. The ugly face of war was not directed on military targets any more. Instead, they turned the attack to break the spirit of civilisation. The bombing seemed unreal to Marta.

Apart from the injuries she was obviously in a state of shock from the horrors of the past two days and nights. Lying there, she felt so lonely and afraid, but eventually her inherent spirit to survive returned and after a while she was able to leave the hospital. To find what…?

Heavy and weak she walked from the hospital, which being hidden by many tall trees had escaped damage. Now she saw the destruction before her: fragments of houses which had been shattered, the gaunt burnt-out skeletons standing out defiantly against the sky after battle.

A few haggard people were still searching in the hot debris of what had been their homes. The hopeless look on their faces said it all. She felt their feelings and desolation in her own heart. What was she going to find when she reached what had been her home?

Finally she arrived at her street, or what was left of it. The buildings were all destroyed and burnt down. Marta could just see the opening of the cellar. She could not resist squeezing through into the passage below to see what had happened to the things she had stored there.

The air was hot and humid and the dust made her cough and

choke. She wanted to be sick: her crippled stomach was still very sensitive to such treatment. All that was left was the black skeleton of her bike and the metal parts of her record player. The records still looked so neat, all in a row, but as Marta touched them they collapsed into a heap of ashes. So much for her worldly goods! Once more she had nothing.

A voice brought her back to reality. 'What are you doing down there?' a man asked her. Marta started crying. Exhausted and stressed beyond her limits she sobbed and sobbed.

'Come now, calm yourself,' the man said as he helped her up again. 'Have you nowhere to go?' She shook her head. He took her to a school where people were being sheltered. Women were serving food and drinks to everyone. They asked her name.

'Have you any relations?'

Marta didn't know who was still alive, so she couldn't tell them. She stayed the night with the other people.

The next day she was given some money to travel to Leipzig to Father. 'There have been no air attacks so you will be safe,' she was told.

This place was not a healthy environment. With the heat and bodies lying around under rubble the rats became a real pest.

To Be or Not to Be

THE JOURNEY TO LEIPZIG WAS TEDIOUS AND NOT VERY CLEAR in Marta's memory. Everything seemed so different. She remembered war being declared and all the things that had happened since then. Now she was returning, a refugee crippled with pains in her stomach and confusion in her mind.

Her father welcomed her with open arms again. He was now married to Maria, a long-time friend who had always shown him a great deal of kindness and love. Although Marta never thought of her as a step-mother, she quite liked her. They showed great understanding of Marta's confused feelings and poor health. They too had suffered heartache. Klara, beautiful Klara, was dead. Their flat was completely destroyed and her husband was missing, presumed dead. There was still no news of Heinrich, so her father had indeed plenty to worry about.

The authorities in Leipzig showed a great deal of compassion to Marta's plight. She was given money and coupons for clothes and food. She needed time to reclaim her senses and recover from her ordeals.

Four months later, just as she was gradually getting stronger, her life once more was at the mercy of the enemy.

She was awakened one night by her father shaking her.

'Didn't you hear the air raid sirens? Get up and dress quickly,' he commanded.

Actually, he was a warden of the block of flats and had to make sure all the people in his care were safely down in the cellars. Marta did not hurry – she could not hear a sound outside and after the terrible raids on Hamburg it seemed to her that it was a false alarm. If only she was a medium, for with premonition she might have sensed the danger.

Suddenly she heard the droning of a plane, a hissing noise and a crash followed by the sound of the plane gaining height and going away. It seemed very uncanny to Marta – so different to anything she had experienced before.

She began to hurry now, packing a few belongings in a bag. Just as she was going out of the room her father entered the flat short of breath and looking very annoyed at Marta's casual behaviour.

Then a strange noise made them both listen. An ominously crackling sound was heard. Her father parted the thick, heavy curtains and they stared disbelievingly at the sight outside. There was a glow all around them.

'The house is on fire,' her father gasped.

A crash in the kitchen made Marta run in there to see what was happening. To her horror the ceiling had fallen in and there was burning debris everywhere.

They tried fighting the fire with buckets of water, but they could not stop it from spreading. Burning wood was falling around her father's head, and Marta could smell his hair singing. He threw some water over his head and Marta shouted, 'Come out of here, Father, before we are burnt alive in this furnace!'

His clothes were scorching as Marta urged him out of the flat. Once outside he had the idea of a human chain to pass water up to control the fire, but this was impossible. The phosphorous canister destroyed the flats as thoroughly as an explosive bomb would have done, but at least with this fire system there was a better chance of survival for people in the building.

The stunned occupants watched as everything they had strived for over many years burnt to the ground. They were shivering in the bitter cold December morning, not able to believe what they saw. Marta looked at her father. He looked like a clown ready to go on stage. His hair was frozen in a grotesque kind of way, standing stiffly up, and his suit was frozen too. With his smoke-blackened face he looked so pitiful. '*Lache Bajazzo*,' the irony of it all... A dear old lady offered her father and his wife part of a very large flat nearby.

Kind people offered many gifts to help replace some of the essential things they had lost. The authorities were also very helpful again, but Marta had been in Leipzig long enough and decided that she was going back to Hamburg to find out if by a miracle Mutti, Hanne and Kate were alive somewhere in the ruined city.

Uncle Heini is Found Safe

MARTA HAD NO ILLUSIONS ABOUT WHAT SHE WOULD FIND, remembering her last view of the devastation. Her father understood that she wanted to go back now that she felt able to cope with the situation, but he impressed upon her the fact that she could always return to Leipzig and live with them. Soon she was on her way back once more.

After her six-month absence she was amazed at the transformed scene that greeted her. A town hall, churches and a shopping centre were standing amidst the ruins. Local trains were in working order, and the thought crossed her mind that it might be a good idea to travel to Uncle Heini's.

As the train approached the rural area where he lived Marta was pleased to see her hunch seemed right; nothing had disturbed this country district.

Walking up the flight of stairs to their flat, she wondered how they would react to her unannounced appearance.

Aunty Julia opened the door and looked startled, as if she was looking at a ghost.

'It's Marta,' she called out.

Uncle Heini appeared. 'Come in, come in,' he said in his gentle voice. The flat was warm and she was given food and a hot drink. There was such a lot to talk about. They had tried without success to trace Mutti or Marta. They really were so glad that she was alive.

They offered her the sofa to sleep on as their spare room had been taken over by the authorities to accommodate homeless people.

After a night's sleep Marta went back again to her own district, but it seemed unfamiliar. Some people had made their homes under the ruins of houses and flats in cellars which had survived the destruction down to the ground. She went around asking people with the hope that someone had heard Mutti's name, but on and on Marta walked the street. There was no trace of Mutti or Kate.

On the third day of her search she was walking in a main street going away from her old district, with shops newly established. People were queuing up for food. Suddenly Marta stared at a figure looking into a shop window. Her hair was not brown but grey. Could it be Mutti? She started running in fear the figure would disappear like an illusion. Her heart was beating fast as the woman turned to face her.

'Oh, Mutti! Where have you been?' she cried out as they fell into each others arms crying. As the people in the queue witnessed this emotional reunion, they too cried unashamedly.

'Where are you staying?' Marta wanted to know.

Mutti took her to the place where she was now living, if it could be described as that.

'Oh my God!' was all that Marta could say as they entered a damp, smelly cellar and went into a dark little room lit by a solitary candle. There was a box for a table and a hard bench to sleep on with only two blankets for cover. This very depressing sight overshadowed the joy of finding Mutti again.

Next to this was another small room occupied by Kate and her daughter. Over a drink Marta began to piece together the events which had followed the first holocaust. Mutti had fled with Kate, her daughter and parents in wagons provided for refugees fleeing the city. They had gone to a farm belonging to relatives of Kate's before they eventually came back and found the cellar to live in. Marta thought it was a degrading existence.

They had searched for Marta and the lodger. The lodger's burned skeleton was found in the rubble, Mutti told her. They assumed she was dead as well as time passed, but Marta was saved in the nick of time, as it became apparent.

'Why didn't you go to Uncle Heini? He is your brother,' Marta asked her. 'He searched for you in our district, not this one,' she remarked. 'He thought you were dead as well as myself.'

Mutti couldn't give Marta an answer to this.

Her daughter could only assume that the shock of everything had prevented her mother from behaving rationally. She told them all what had happened to herself.

What can I do now? Marta wondered to herself. She could not stay at Uncle Heini's indefinitely, not wishing to intrude upon their lives. They already had the refugees to cope with. Mutti looked so small and lost, like some down-and-out; she couldn't leave her again. Marta felt she had no choice but to join Mutti in the cellar.

When Marta arrived at her uncle and aunt's home she told them that she had found Mutti and would be living with her, but she could not bring herself to mention the dreadful condition that her mother was existing in. She could see that they were as puzzled as she had been. Why had Mutti not contacted them at all? They shared the same opinion as Marta that it must have been a reaction to the shock she had suffered.

She stayed the night with her uncle and aunt and the next morning left to go back to the city. She promised to take Mutti to visit them one weekend.

As she left the warm and cosy flat to settle into a damp hole in the ruins of the city her heart sank, but not her spirit. She must try and boost Mutti's demoralised mind. She herself was young, and even after all she had been through she seemed to go on and on like a rubber ball on a rough sea, bouncing up and down at the will of the waves with no friendly island in sight to provide the respite and salvation she was searching for.

Putting on a brave face, Marta went to a school across the road from her new 'home' where she was issued with two blankets, a ration book and money. Her name was then put down for registration. Then she spent her time searching among the ruins for anything useful. She found a steel bed half buried – just what she needed! It took quite a while to get it out and drag it through the entrance of the cellar, and putting it into the right position was quite a problem as it rained through the rubble and the place became waterlogged, so stepping stones were placed around the bed.

Surprisingly she found quite a selection of cups, saucers etc., as she carefully excavated amongst the rubble – the contents of what had once graced the interiors of the flats before their destruction.

To Marta's mind the thing she hated most was being so vulnerable, because anyone could just walk into the cellar. The door had no strength or protection and the small windows she boarded up shut out what little light there was. The rats were everywhere. Oh, how she loathed those creatures!

It was not surprising that she soon found herself a stray cat. She would share her rations with it and in return the cat would chase the rats away. Besides, she had something to love and cuddle and to be of comfort to her in her lonely existence.

They had found Mutti a job again cleaning a school. Mutti had saved some sentimental belongings of Hans's when she was evacuated: his special uniform; dagger; hat and the waldxitta he played as well.

Surrender

ADVANCING ALLIED FORCES WERE CLOSING IN ON HAMBURG as Admiral von Dönitz announced the shocking news of Hitler's death. As the Admiral had been appointed the new leader, he declared it was his first duty to end the useless killings. He gave orders for all fighting units to lay down their arms in unconditional surrender.

On 8 May, all arms were laid down, and the thousands of war-weary German soldiers walked the bitter way of defeat into prisoner-of-war camps.

As for the people of Germany, they bowed their heads in silence to the brave soldiers imprisoned or killed in action for their sacrifices. Their sons were dead. At home there was no *wiedersehn*. Millions of dead covered the earth. Once beautiful cities were destroyed all over Europe. Farmlands had been ravaged by the armies and airforces. Refugees, the homeless and hungry were everywhere. So many people were dead at the home front, maimed or homeless. Others, like Marta, were just about existing. The future looked bleak.

For all this we have the Führer to thank, Marta thought bitterly.

Aftermath: Humiliation

A CURFEW WAS PUT INTO FORCE AS THE BRITISH FORCES occupied Hamburg. *Peace at last, nothing can harm us any more*, thought Marta, as the army of occupation mingled in the streets with the German people.

Close by her cellar home was a large hospital which the British took over. Many German people found jobs there; even Mutti was tempted to work in the kitchens.

'What about the pension you will get from the school cleaning job you done for years?' Marta asked, trying to guide her to do the best thing. 'You have to think about it carefully, Mutti.'

Marta had noticed how frail her mother looked and realised that moving desks and chairs around was heavy work for her. Besides, Mutti had a point; a friend who was working in the hospital kitchens showed her some chocolate, dried milk and coffee: tempting luxuries. Her pension years were still a long way off, and food was important now. In the end Marta was quite pleased when her mother did get a job at the hospital, and she loved it.

For Marta, her most humiliating experience was still to come...

One night as she lay in bed she heard loud voices and heavy footsteps coming into the cellar. She heard banging on doors, and a loud command of, 'Open up!' She was scared out of her wits. There was more banging and repeated orders to 'Open up.' The doors were not strong enough to withstand this treatment, so Marta got out of bed and partly opened her door.

Instantly two British military policemen pushed past her, shining their torches over the room. Cold and frightened, Marta asked them what they were looking for. 'British soldiers,' they replied. After they realised that there were just terrified women in the cellar she was told to get dressed.

'Why?' she wanted to know.

'You will see,' one of them replied abruptly. The other policeman then told Kate to do the same. The one left in Marta's room started to looked around. His torchlight lit the dagger and hat hanging under Hans's photograph. Grinning with pleasure he took them off the wall and walked out, telling her to hurry up. She pleaded with him not to take these treasured possessions – it was all they had in remembrance of Hans – but the policeman ignored her pleas and tears. She felt so defenceless, but underneath burned a furious anger against this common thief.

Meanwhile, Kate was dressed and her weeping child was handed over to a petrified Mutti to care for. With no explanation Marta and Kate were told to get into a jeep outside.

Speeding through the streets they arrived at a big building in the city. They were hustled into the building and told to wait.

There were a few other woman sitting on benches looking as scared as Marta and Kate felt. After a while a door opened and a white-coated man beckoned Marta to come inside. He was a doctor and asked her a lot of questions. From this conversation she learnt the reason why she was being handled in such a way. Someone had reported them to the police, accusing them of having sexual relations with British soldiers. That is why the military police had swooped at night, hoping to catch them in bed together.

'But no one was there,' Marta indignantly denied the charges, and said that she had no intentions of ever doing so.

The doctor still told her to get undressed ready to be examined for any sexual diseases. She was not a teenager, but her knowledge of such diseases was nil. She didn't even know they existed or the danger they contained. That examination was the most embarrassing experience to her sensitive and innocent mind. The shame of it all she never would forget. The doctor confirmed that she was clean and could go... Kate too was cleared.

They stood outside the unknown building far from home. It was past midnight and they had no money to travel back. They had a long, long walk ahead of them through the silent streets. The thought of ending her miserable life crossed Marta's mind as she thought of the dreadful ordeal she had been through. Poor Kate, she looked like a ghost and was trembling in the cold night.

Self pity is no good, Marta thought to herself. *What of all the dead who lie beneath the earth, silent and grotesque in the darkness of no return?* She was alive; she had been spared. There must be a reason for that.

The outcome of the unjustified degrading treatment was shown in Marta's actions the next day. She decided to find herself a big Alsatian dog who was fearless enough to protect her with his life. She trusted animals far more than she did humans.

A kennel was found and with a few cigarettes Mutti had bought home from soldiers she'd done some sewing for, a deal was made. To keep an Alsatian on food rations was a problem, but she pocketed her pride and went to several butchers begging for bones and scraps. Sometimes they were good enough to make a soup for Marta and Mutti as well as Sherry the Alsatian.

A Canoe called Peterle

A WARM SUNNY MORNING GREETED MARTA COMING OUT OF the damp, musty cellar one weekend, so she decided that she would have a day out to see about her canoe and go for a peaceful trip on the canal. Before the bombing of Hamburg she had scraped and saved to buy a second-hand canoe, which was stored in a boathouse at Winterhude on the outskirts of Hamburg.

Packing a snack to eat she told Sherry to be on guard.

When she arrived at the boathouse near the canal she greeted the attendant there cheerfully. 'Lovely day, isn't it?' she said to him. 'Will you give me a hand launching Peterle?'

He didn't respond to her, but looked serious and glum.

'What's the matter?' Marta asked him.

'I am sorry, love, but your canoe has gone.'

'How come? What do you mean by that?' she queried.

He told her that a couple of British soldiers had come to the boathouse and just commanded a canoe for a day out. They had pointed to Peterle, which was Marta's canoe, and told him to put in the water for them. They had gone off and he had never seen them or the canoe again.

'If it is any consolation to you, yours is not the only one missing,' he told Marta.

Seeing the horrified and angry look on her face, he advised her to report it to the German waterpolice. 'They may just have left it somewhere on the bank of a river, after the novelty had worn off,' the man added.

My one remaining pleasure taken from me! Her mind went back to happier times cruising down the river with weeping willows overhanging the banks where you could stop at a sheltered spot and relax at peace with nature. *Now this*! *There is no end to it.*

After the destruction of all her belongings during the war she hadn't expected to have this happen now they were at peace! The forces of occupation seemed to think that they could take whatever they fancied from people. Some German girls made it easy for them and for the price of a few cigarettes were available to play their games. Marta watched as some of these girls went by in canoes paddled by British soldiers.

Where is Peterle now? she wondered as she sadly made her way home again. She had never thought there was a possibility that from now on nothing belonged to the people who had lost the war. Embittered by another blow from the victorious liberators, she hastened back to the smelly, damp cellar to hide her grief and hurt.

She found Kate outside amongst the ruins sitting in a sheltered corner enjoying the warm sunshine. Marta collapsed onto the rubble beside her and poured out the sorry story of the missing canoe. Finally her emotions got the better of her and tears welled up in anger and hatred. Real charmers the British – nothing seemed sacred to them. Oh, she had a lot to learn!

Another Reunion

WITH THE PASSING OF TIME THINGS GRADUALLY IMPROVED. Homes were rebuilt as the rubble was cleared away and shops started to have more to sell.

News came from Father that Heinrich was a prisoner of war, but of Hans they heard nothing.

Marta went out once more searching for a job. She went to the factory where she had last worked, but it was just debris. On the other side she could see people working in a building. *Hanne used to work there*, she thought. *I wonder...*

The whole building was intact, so she decided to go over and investigate. Carefully she opened a door and peered inside. There were a lot of women around and she could hear that they were talking in a different language. An old man stood there watching her. She went over to him and asked, 'Who are these foreign women?'

'Russian prisoners,' he told her.

She thought he was kidding.

'They will be going home soon,' he said. 'They are only a nuisance here.'

Marta then began to talk about her friend who used to work at this complex.

'She may still be here,' the old fellow remarked. 'There, upstairs,' he pointed, 'is a medical department. The young woman working there may know something about your friend.'

'Oh, thank you very much for your help,' Marta replied, and made her way up the stairs to the room he had pointed out to her. She knocked on the door and waited.

'Come in,' called a familiar voice. As she opened the door the young woman turned around and facing her now was her long-lost friend, Hanne.

'Oh, Marta!' She was astonished and delighted to see her. 'I wondered if I would ever see you again,' she said, hugging her old friend.

'What a coincidence finding you like this,' Marta said.

At last something nice had happened!

Hanne explained that she had been evacuated with her parents, but that they had recently returned and were now living in a prefab nearby; a very different district from their old one. They too had lost everything, and her fiancé had been killed in action. Her wedding dress and a chest full of items which she had carefully saved up for were also destroyed.

Finding each other again meant a great deal to both Marta and Hanne. Little did they know that fate was to link their future lives in a most extraordinary way...

Unsafe Condition

LIFE SEEMED TO BE LOOKING MORE PROMISING AS MARTA strolled under shady trees in a nearby park away from the gloom of the cellar. The beauty of the flower garden and the fragrant scent of the roses in the air soothed her aching heart and the past receded to the back of her mind. Girls in flowered dresses enjoyed the attention paid them by British soldiers.

Finding Hanne again had been a blessing. Now she was not a solitary person, things would be so different. The future began to hold hope at last.

Another improvement came with the authorities finding new accommodation for all the people living in unhealthy conditions. A report was handed in stating that the cellars were appalling and dangerous. A most welcome letter arrived to inform them that rooms close by had been allocated to Marta, Mutti and Kate with her daughter, stating the dates each person could enter.

What an improvement this will be, thought Marta. *To live in a dry place, with the luxury of a bathroom and toilet...* she would definitely call that progress!

Mutti had improved tremendously and was very happy in her new work. She urged Marta to take a job at the hospital, but she could not yet bring herself to work for the ex-enemy. Was it pride, or did she feel guilty because she would be collaborating with them? As the saying goes, if you can't beat them, join them...

Finally Marta convinced herself that it wouldn't harm anyone now, and plucked up the courage to ask for a job. She turned pale at the suggestion she work as a cleaner. Proudly she declined the offer, and left the office walking through the hospital grounds to the exit.

She received a lot of attention from passing soldiers. Remarks of, 'Hi, Ginger! Got a date to spare?' followed her, and wolf whistles pierced her ears as she hastened through the gate to more familiar ground.

She looked in shops to calm herself. At least she had not lost her feminine attraction!

The town was full of foreigners, and when Marta went shopping with Hanne they quite enjoyed the attention they attracted. With Hanne there Marta felt more relaxed. After all, they hadn't lost their appreciation of being admired, even if they had lost their youth!

In the meantime the moving was getting underway. Kate and her daughter were the first to go. Marta helped Kate to carry her few worldly goods across to a flat nearby.

Not a very large room for the two of them, Marta thought. Well, beggars can't be choosers, as the saying goes. At least it was dry and safe, which was a great asset to be much appreciated.

Mutti soon followed into an even smaller room, with very little light coming from a small window.

Marta was luckier; she got a fairly large room on the third floor of a council house. Her landlady was a middle-aged widow who didn't exactly welcome this intruder with open arms. She made all sorts of rules and there were many regulations to be obeyed. First of all she refused to have the Alsatian in her home. Marta's heart sank, but she knew in her heart that she had no choice in the matter. 'Well, Sherry,' she said to her protector, 'you have to go, but where I just don't know.'

Luck for once was with her that day. Walking along the main street with the dog by her side he often attracted the attention of passers-by, being a beautiful specimen of his breed. On this particular day a lady stopped her and commented on his lovely markings. They had a bitch, but not as beautiful as Sherry.

'How about mating them?' she asked. 'Would you come and see my husband?' the lady enquired. 'I am sure he will be impressed with your dog.'

Nothing to lose, Marta thought, and she went along with her. What a stroke of luck it turned out to be! They had a coal merchant's business, and as Sherry was a very good watchdog the husband there and then offered Marta a very high price for him. What a surprise for her! She had expected to take him to kennels and receive no money for him. Lady Luck was really smiling down on her.

Although she was sad to part with the dog, she knew he had found a good home and a mate. With the money she would be able to buy some furniture for her new home.

She went to that miserable cellar for the last time and packed her few belongings. She left without regrets, happy and relieved to put that part of her troubled life behind her. She walked the short distance to her new room, went across to the window, opened it and leaned out breathing in the air and looking at the world below. *Better get ready*, she thought. *I will be late meeting Hanne*. Pleased with herself, she left for the meeting place.

'You look happy,' Hanne remarked.

Marta told her about the chance meeting which had led to her selling Sherry to a good home and leaving her with cash in hand. 'I'll treat you to an ice cream. How about it?'

'I accept,' Hanne said smiling, and in good spirits they made their way into the city.

English and American music was heard.

'Listen!' Hanne stopped Marta as the voice of Vera Lynn sounded loud and clear.

'Lay down your arms and surrender to mine…'

The city streets were busy, and crowds of people mingled with foreigners as different languages were heard in the shops. English soldiers linked with German girls was now a common sight, and this caused the British concern. Anxious mothers feared for their sons – not to be killed, mind you, but not to be led astray by a German female! So the British forces had their hands full trying to intervene. If a British soldier had honourable intentions towards a German girl and suggested getting married the unfortunate soldier was posted elsewhere. This was the first reaction to such foolish notions: out of sight, out of mind.

If posting was not always possible due to other factors, then when applying for permission, like Hanne's soldier had to do to his commanding officer, there was delayed action in the paperwork. The proposed bride had to have a medical by a British doctor and her past medical and private life was checked thoroughly.

In the case of Hanne and Jimmy it took nine long months to get their papers through, and finally permission was granted for them to marry. The wedding was arranged by the forces and was very formal.

Marta commented to Hanne, 'If it took so long to decide a German subject was fit to be married to a British soldier then they must hold a high regard for themselves!'

Hanne looked thoughtful.

Marta kept on, 'I hope you know what you are letting yourself in for.' But on a more cheerful note she added, 'Well, let's hope love will triumph above all.' Hanne smiled at that.

Life seemed like a merry-go-round: war and destruction; mixing with foreigners – it was all just part of growing up.

A Lucky Meeting

As it happened, that day also turned out to be of great importance to Hanne. Two British soldiers started to trail them, and when they caught them up they asked the girls if they would go to the pictures with them. Questioningly Hanne looked at Marta, who shrugged her shoulders. She could see that her friend wanted to accept the invitation and so they ended up in a cinema, seeing their first English film and eating chocolate.

Afterwards with promises to meet again they parted. Marta could see that Hanne was quite impressed but she was not, and told Hanne so.

While Hanne was courting Marta decided to go to the hospital to try for a job once more. This time a man was in the office. He looked up as she asked for a job.

'Do you speak English?' he asked her.

With instant bravado, Marta said, 'Yes.'

'Put her into the officers' quarters,' he told the secretary and left the office.

She took down Marta's particulars and said, 'Start on Monday morning.'

Marta couldn't believe her luck! She was employed at last. *Wait till Mutti hears about this*, she thought joyfully.

Meantime Hanne was to get married in August and she followed her husband over to England in November.

Monday morning found Marta in a very anxious state. She met Mutti and they walked together to the British Military Hospital. Marta reported at the office and was taken over to a ward. Above this was the officers' quarters. A woman present was told to show her what her duties would be. It turned out that she was to be a sort of batman (or woman) to eight medical officers.

She had to wake them with an early cup of tea, clean their shoes and after they had left for the officers' mess she made the beds. The other woman did the cleaning of the rooms while Marta had to polish the buttons and pips of their uniforms.

This turned out to be her daily task, and her training at that memorable camp years ago stood her in good stead now. No problems arose between her and the other woman; they worked well together as a team.

Marta found it rather embarrassing to enter the room of each officer first thing in the morning, but the officers – mostly doctors or dentists – were of course gentlemen who treated her with great respect.

Marta was well aware of her position and did her job thoroughly to the great satisfaction of the officers. Their relationship was one of mutual understanding. Marta's life took on a new meaning with self-respect, new interest and a new language to learn.

Her first wages were spent on a second-hand radio. English papers and magazines she took home to study, and this way she learned how to read and spell as well as to speak English. The officers helped her a great deal and praised her for learning so quickly.

One day she took a phone call for an officer. After she had said he was not present the caller asked if they could leave a message. She didn't understand and put the phone down.

The first officer, who returned to his room, called her to do a job for him. Bravely she asked him what a message meant. He explained, but better still he handed her a small dictionary.

'Here you are – you will find all your answers in there,' he said. It turned out to be her most valued possession for her future life.

'Thank you, sir,' she said gratefully.

At night she listened to the BFN, learning from songs such as 'Don't Fence me In' or, 'You are my Sunshine' and many more popular songs from that time.

At the weekend, beside her pay she received a bonus from the officers for looking after their personal laundry, not money but coffee, cigarettes and luxuries she had never seen before came into her possession. Marta decided to do better and try to sell some of these on the black market. Rations of food were still very meagre and she wanted to get more for herself and Mutti.

Adaptation Essential

THE USUAL CRY OF 'HOW ABOUT THE PICTURES TONIGHT, Ginger?' was always laughed off by Marta. *Really*, she thought, *it's almost impossible to find a sensible fellow among this lot!*

They were mostly too young to be even considered for a night out in Marta's mind.

In her environment at the hospital Marta learned a great deal about English customs at Christmas time. She went into work as usual, but after she went into the first officer's room to give him his morning tea, he cheerfully wished her 'Merry Christmas' and from under the bed he retrieved a box of Scottish shortcake and handed it to her.

'Thank you, sir,' she said in a surprised manner.

Each officer gave her a present, and soon her workroom looked like Father Christmas's den. She had never received so many gifts in her life!

At lunchtime, as the officers returned to their quarters, they invited Marta to have a drink to celebrate Christmas. Not wanting to offend them after their kindness to her, she accepted. Carefully she sipped a little (remembering her downfall and the suffering she had endured the next day).

'Come on now,' the friendly captain persuaded.

She tried to explain that alcohol did not suit her sensitive stomach, but they assured her that what she was drinking wouldn't harm anyone. Actually it was whisky and she had never heard of it before. It needed very little to make her intoxicated for only the second time in her life.

The phone was ringing and she could hardly stagger to it. Lifting the receive she leaned against the wall and slowly sank down to a sitting position, leaving the phone hanging in mid-air with a voice calling out of it. Her workmate Berta found her there and helped her up, saying, 'It's time for you to go home!'

Helping her into her outdoor clothes and putting some gifts

into her bag, she put her arm around her and left the quarters to take her home. Fortunately she was a very strong woman, a bit like Hilde at Marien Hof.

Placing Marta's bag onto the table at the checkout for inspection she waited while the soldier examined the contents.

'Where did you get all this?' she was asked after the initial gasp of astonishment at the sight of all the presents. Her friend was not amused. In fact, she was rather annoyed with the trouble Marta was causing her. She told the soldier to phone the officers' quarters to verify that Marta had been given the presents. This they did and then the two of them were allowed to go home. Marta could not remember much about the incident, or the next day. She was too ill to move.

When she reported back for duty the day after that her workmate was very relieved to see her. Marta found out at the officers' mess that there was going to be a party that night and the staff were invited. Although she was still under the weather she thought that it would be great fun and was looking forward to it.

After work she went home to get dolled up, as the saying goes, ready to return to the officers' mess party.

The staff sat at tables while the officers served them with food and drinks (nothing strong for Marta, of course). She tried a glass of champagne and got light-headed just with one glass! She was merrily chatting to a major when a young lieutenant asked her for a dance. The major winked in the direction of the young man.

'Watch yourself,' he whispered, looking amused.

Marta was not at all shy dancing with her superior. In fact, she had great fun all evening and was even chauffeured home by an officer. This caused a lot of tongue-wagging for a while, entirely without reason.

Mutti was transferred to the kitchen below the officers' quarters, and when the soldiers found out that Marta was her daughter they bribed her with chocolate to try and get a date, but Marta wasn't all that bothered, though she did occasionally go out with a soldier from the ward below.

Teddy

THE NEXT YEAR A NEW OFFICER ARRIVED WITH A PROBLEM; A little bitch with puppies. He asked Marta could she help; of course, no problem! Plenty of space about and they thrived under Marta's care, and after eight weeks Marta had the pick of the litter. The rest were given to other people.

Soon after this Marta was taking Drixy, as the bitch was called, along with her to the shops. Just as they passed a cinema the doors flew open and the crowd came rushing outside. Drixy went missing. Either she got mixed up in the crowds and got lost or took fright and ran away; no one will ever know. Marta searched for her for hours, but there was no sign of the little dog and she was very depressed about this. She was also very worried about telling the officer what had happened, but fortunately he wasn't upset about it because he was returning to England very shortly, so it was a blessing in disguise.

Teddy, as she called her little pup, was a bundle of joy. Thank goodness he was so tiny, because she had to take him to work every day in her shopping bag, hoping he would not pop his head out at the wrong time and be spotted! Once in the hospital if anyone asked about the dog she would say that he belonged to an officer.

Meanwhile, Marta learnt a lot about the British forces working in close contact with them.

When the day's work was done all German staff had to report to a building next to the gate where their bags were searched by the British soldiers for anything belonging to the hospital.

Friendly Persuasion

SUMMERTIME MADE LIFE WORTH LIVING. SWIMMING OR JUST lazing in the sun, taking Teddy for long walks Marta felt at peace with the world at last. The past was put behind her and the future beckoned. Life seemed good and she was very happy working at the hospital.

One day Teddy escaped inside the hospital and ran into the ward looking for Mutti.

'Come here, Teddy!' Marta shouted. A soldier picked him up and handed him to her.

'Thank you,' she said, noticing that she had never seen this young soldier before.

After that she saw him quite often. He seemed to spend a lot of time near the stairway, smiling at her as she passed through. She asked Mutti about this newcomer.

'Oh, he is ever so nice,' Mutti told her. Not like the other lads who walked all over the kitchen floor as soon as she had cleaned it and had it ready for inspection. He had good manners and apologised to Mutti if he had to go in.

After a while he plucked up the courage to ask Marta to go to the cinema with him. She accepted, on the strength of Mutti's remark about him.

They enjoyed the film which was called *It's Magic* – it was the first glimpse of Doris Day for Marta. She found out that his name was Stuart, and sure enough he was very well behaved, and this was much appreciated by Marta.

They met quite often, sometimes going to the Stadt park with Teddy in attendance and having a lot of fun.

One morning, going to work as usual with Teddy in her bag, Marta passed a group of soldiers on parade. Suddenly Teddy lifted his head and jumped out of the bag, running towards the soldiers with Marta in hot pursuit. His tail wagging, the dog went between the lines, sniffing at the soldiers until he found the one he was looking for. He jumped up as Stuart stood there to attention pretending he did not know him. The sergeant told Marta to get hold of her dog as he was causing a distraction.

Blushing like a beetroot because of all the remarks the soldiers made to her she picked Teddy up and made a hasty departure.

'How could you do this to me?' she scolded him. And Stuart had to endure the remarks of his mates: 'Now we know who is going out with Ginger! You are a sly one!'

Unfortunately, going home one night, Teddy ran into the road before Marta could stop him. There was a screech of brakes as a car tried to avoid him, but he was hit and the little dog ran back to her whimpering, but she could see no injury. She could tell that something was wrong with him internally, and the next day she asked one of the officers if he could do anything for Teddy. It was too late, and the little dog died later that day. Stuart tried to console Marta over her sad loss. He too had liked Teddy and felt upset about it.

Stuart's attention somehow had a soothing effect on her, she noticed. He was of a reserved nature and very serious minded, much older than his years. By now Marta was well aware that he was younger than herself, and she felt sure that nothing would come of their harmless friendship. She told him about her past, her sorrow and the grievances of her heart, and he seemed abatable in his support for her.

Then she dated another soldier. Stuart heard about it and said he wanted to talk to her. Marta said casually, 'Meet you tonight at the usual place.'

When they met Stuart was not at all his usual calm self.

'What's wrong with you?' Marta asked him.

He looked at her sternly. 'Can't you guess? Why did you go out with another soldier?' He was jealous and hurt.

Marta looked at him. 'You are so young, can't you see?' she was afraid of their age differences. He took her in his arms and kissed her tenderly, then he told her that he was going home on leave, so they didn't see each other for a while.

During this separation Marta realised how she missed him and his calm influence. She felt restless and was glad one morning to see him back working in the ward. She could tell from his face that he felt the same.

He was waiting outside the gates for her and they went to her flat together. As they got to really know each other he found out all about her. He patiently listened, understood and respected her. He was serious about their relationship, and especially so as they became lovers in love...

Marta looked at her horoscope for reassurance. He was Gemini, and according to the stars he was the perfect partner. *Well, we have to see*, she thought, *only time will tell.*

Shared Pleasure

STUART SUGGESTED GOING HORSE RIDING ON THEIR NEXT afternoon off. 'You are kidding!' Marta said, not believing what he had said. 'Where is that possible, Stuart?'

He told her that other soldiers had been to this place.

'Super, I would love to come,' Marta said excitedly. At home she looked for her brother's uniform trousers. *They will have to do*, she muttered to herself. A blouse covered with cardigan completed the outfit. She looked at herself in the mirror. *Not bad for your age*, she agreed with her image. Her face was still childlike and a great asset.

She was in high spirits when she met Stuart at the S Bahn station. He looked at her lovingly as they boarded a train. They sat in silence as the German people in the compartment stared at Marta in disgust. Going out with British soldiers was considered a shameless thing to do. *What a hussy*, they thought, looking her up and down.

Marta felt guilty and embarrassed as they talked in German, making remarks about her. She was glad Stuart did not understand what was being said. They left the train and Marta was happy to go out into the countryside with hardly anybody around to spoil her pleasure.

The riding school was actually near where Uncle Heini lived. After Stuart made the deal for two horses (with cigarettes) they asked, 'Can you ride?'

Stuart and Marta said yes, they could, and two horses were brought out saddled up ready for riding. Quickly they mounted. Someone then said, 'Do you want a guide?'

'No,' they answered, and were shown a track to follow.

'Just go along there; you can't go wrong.'

'Thanks,' Stuart said as they rode away into the countryside. A dream come true – just the two of them together riding in nature's own environment. Marta was overjoyed and very excited. Stuart was his usual placid self, but he did look happy and pleased at finding out about the riding school. Happiness is sharing pleasures, magic moments.

Joyfully Marta urged her horse into a gallop, racing ahead of Stuart and calling him to catch up with her. The gentle breeze was playing with her long red hair. Her cheeks were flushed with this excitement. Their hands met as the horses rode close together.

'Oh, Stuart, I wish we could do this forever,' she said tenderly. 'I am so happy.'

This moment of bliss was so very special to Marta, who feared this happiness could again be taken away from her. *Live now, pay later*, she thought to herself.

Another ride was planned but turned sour because Stuart brought a mate of his; he hadn't the heart to refuse him.

The horses seemed very frisky and needed more controlling. They got out on the trail approaching a gate with an iron frame above it. Stuart and Marta rode through without any trouble, but as they looked back, they saw the other fellow hanging from the frame while the horse walked from under him. It was a funny sight, really. Stuart caught the horse and once more his pal was helped into the saddle. He hadn't told Stuart that he had never sat on a horse before. He was a Londoner.

Oh great, thought Marta, as they had to go at a walking pace.

On the way back some children had left a bicycle fallen down on a bridge they had to cross. Stuart's pal didn't seem to notice it. His horse was startled by it and took off with him hanging on desperately. Then the horse reared, throwing the rider to the ground where he lay motionless. The horse, free of the rider, started running for home. To make matters worse Marta saw a big Alsatian dog getting rather close to them. Her horse started to play up, so she decided to dismount.

She was just in time because her horse reared, and ripping the reins out of her hands, galloped after the other horse.

Marta ran over to the motionless figure on the ground. He was ashen and in pain; in fact he had a dislocated collarbone.

With Stuart's help he got up and slowly they made their way back to the stables. The staff were just setting out to find out what had happened to them; three horses arriving back without their riders had certainly alarmed them!

Stuart and Marta never went riding there again.

A Band of Gold

THEY SPENT THEIR TIME TOGETHER DISCOVERING LOVE IN their innocent way. Soon Stuart was going to be demobbed and would be returning home to England. He spoke to Mutti about getting engaged to her daughter, asking for permission, kind of.

'Of course!' She loved the lad and was happy to think of him as her son-in-law. Marta had found Mr Right at last. Who would have thought that Mr Right would be an English soldier? Life is strange at times, and fate has many surprises in store for people. Some are pleasant, some are not. Marta surely had received her share of the latter.

They started to look in jewellery shops for a ring. The German custom was that both partners wear a wedding ring. Getting engaged the rings were worn on the left hand and on the wedding day they changed them onto the right hand.

A ring was found for Marta. Stuart was an English man and not wearing one.

A little party was arranged at Marta's flat. There Stuart put the ring on Marta's finger with a promise to marry her as soon as possible.

A visit with Stuart to see Uncle Heini and Aunty Julia was arranged. They were very impressed by his good manners and politeness. They wished them good luck and happiness in their future together.

The day of Stuart's departure from Marta and Hamburg dawned. As they clung to one another for the last time he told her that as soon as he had saved enough money for her fare he would send for her and they would get married in England.

As they parted waving their last goodbye, Marta thought that here was the man she had learnt to love leaving her, but she did not break down in despair. Instead she felt calm and assured that they would meet again. *Don't know where, don't know when, but I know we'll meet again some sunny day...*

Such was his power. He could be trusted to keep his promise.

Arriving at Harwich

SUDDENLY MARTA HEARD BELLS RINGING AND PEOPLE shouting. Reality hit, she came to her senses, moved quickly, dressed, gathered her meek belongings and went out of her cabin door to find the other girls in the crowds that by now were filling the gangways ready for disembarkation.

Anxiety mingled with tension over what would happen next as the girls gathered around Marta. It seemed their presence gave her moral support and an authoritative status. Without further ado they disembarked with identify cards at the ready to find their contact on the mainland.

A well-informed man stepped forward, formalities were exchanged and they followed him to a waiting bus and were soon travelling through beautiful countryside towards London.

A new country with a different language and nearer to Stuart without his knowledge! Warm feelings enclosed Marta's body, but the moment of attention, of facing reality arrived at Sloane Square, their destination.

A big house faced them and again a man stood at the stairs talking to the driver, but without further delay Marta was told to come inside with her party.

Big rooms faced them with beds and quite quickly each chose one and they were then told to come downstairs for more information.

Having volunteered as German citizens for work in Britain, they had to have an injection in the afternoon, but lunch was the next item on the agenda.

So far so good, Marta thought. Sure enough, a bus arrived again to take them to a hospital. Marta had her work cut out translating for the girls. She also asked the reason for the injection. Casually the explained it was to test for T.B.

Pause for thought. It was the weekend, so the man in charge gave them half a crown to spend in London. Marta was looking for a paper shop to get cards to inform Hanne and Stuart of her new address. The shopkeeper was very helpful with the stamps and she posted them right away. Very pleased with her first deal in English she walked back to the house. Imagining people would look at her being a stranger she was relieved no one took any notice. The tense conditions started to relax. A girl called Gerda asked Marta, 'Do you know anyone in London?'

'No,' she said, and she had no interest in seeing the town.

But the girl kept on and on and in the end Marta reluctantly looked in her little black book. Yes, there was someone she met at her engagement to Stuart, a soldier who was present at the hospital in Hamburg who gave her the address.

'Let's find him.'

'And then what?'

Gerda was not easily put off, and the next thing they were looking for the underground asking people until eventually they found the very street.

It was a Saturday, and like a miracle there was a tall chap coming towards the girls. 'Let's ask him.'

Unbelievably he recognised Marta.

'Hallo, Ginger. What you doing here?'

'Well, Derek, that is rather embarrassing to explain…'

'Well,' he replied, 'I was just going to meet my mate for the pictures,' and without any fuss he offered them his arm. This couldn't be real. It was like fiction…

Next thing another lad took Gerda's arm, and in the dark of the cinema they enjoyed a very interesting film: *Bitter Spring,* never seen before and never forgotten. The world outside didn't exist until they stepped outside into the sunlight.

'Oh my God, what time is it?' They had to be in by nine o'clock.

Like gentlemen they obeyed and the girls were soon safe at the corner of their lodgings. Standing awhile chatting about this episode, Marta saw Derek's face change colour as he stared at something. As she followed his gaze it was she who changed colour; there in the flesh stood Stuart.

She cried as her arms were around him, but he was angry: newly in London and already with fellows! As soon as he recognised Derek all was well and it was a blessing in disguise. Derek took Stuart to his place for the night.

Before Marta was leaving he told her he had been granted the next day – Sunday – off to spend with her. Oh boy! He looked great in civil suit, and he loved her!

Hand in hand they walked away from the prying eyes at the window. Out of sight they embraced and with a tender kiss made up.

What could they do now? Out came Hanne's address. 'Let's find her.' Into the tube station they went. Stuart was in charge, she was just looking at this handsome fellow holding her hand...

'Here you are,' the bus driver told him and they stopped.

Another coincidence! Someone on the other side of the road by the bus stop shouted, 'Marta!' There stood Hanne with her husband on their way to London to see her! What a loving response from Hanne, despite her being heavily pregnant.

Hanne looked at Stuart and was very impressed with Marta's choice, then she had a confession to make about her living standards. They were very primitive; in an old farm building. As Hanne had always lived in a rather posh place and was spoiled, she did not tell her parents, she just lied. Marta was quite impressed about her being so brave, coming to an old farm house in Kent.

Now to climb the dark stairs into a small room with an old, big table and little space around it. Even the window was not giving much light to cheer the place up, but the welcome was friendly as ever. Soon a hot cup of tea and cake were on the table and happiness filled the room. After three years' absence there was so much to say all at once, and time was running out. A beautiful dinner was served by Hanne: pork chops with cauliflower and potatoes. Another surprise; her cooking was surprisingly good. Now well fed, Hanne suggested a trip to the pub to Jim. He was a bit surprised, but then the penny dropped.

'Oh, yes, of course!' With a wink and smile he indicated he understood – Marta and Stuart would like to be alone for a while. Marta blushed, but that soon stopped once in Stuart's arms. Heaven on earth dispensed any guilt.

This was precious, a reunion of their love. They had to be

strong, not knowing what the future held for Marta. With flushed faces they accepted another drink and thanked the pair for their excellent hospitality. It seemed the whole place had a warm glow of happiness for all concerned.

Back at the lodgings, Stuart thanked the kind man for trusting him and turning abruptly away so as not to show his emotions, he left to travel all night back to Blackpool.

With a sad heart, Marta lay in her bed, imagining being in his arms.

Tone Vale

THE MONDAY MORNING AFTER BREAKFAST FOUND THE GIRLS on a bus on their way to their first assignment. They were heading to Somerset to a big mental hospital. Marta didn't know what was involved, and had to look in her dictionary for the meaning. She cried, 'Oh, my God!' But there was no choice now. Marta herself was well disciplined so asserted herself.

Her thoughts were interrupted as the bus turned into a big driveway and stopped before a big, foreboding old building – Tone Vale. There was no time to ponder as they were all ushered by the bus driver to the back to collect their belongings and a nurse appeared to take charge of the group. They were led through locked doors along dark, long corridors. It was very depressing and atmospheric and it didn't do the girls any good.

As they came to a hall in front of a big door, they knocked. 'Come in!' The nurse stopped her charges in front of the desk to face the boss.

Formalities were exchanged, with orders for the nurse. Again they followed the leader to doors outside the building. Ahead a new building was in sight, which turned out to be a new nursing home. Each girl got her own room.

Well, that's more like it, Marta mused. It was neatly set up: wardrobe, bed, desk, own sink and nature through the window. Relaxed she sat on her bed, tired after all the rushing around of late, but London was now left behind.

The door flew open and an excited Gerda came in, talking in German about her room and saying that a lot of Germans were working there.

'Well, sounds promising,' Marta replied.

Another girl entered her room, introducing herself as Inge and informed the girls that the evening meal was at six in the restaurant. She would take them over later. She departed.

Quietly Marta packed her belongings into the drawers and

wardrobe. After a wash and having tidied her hair she looked through her window, thinking of Stuart and about this new enterprise. Her thoughts were interrupted as Inge appeared to take them to supper. Again they went through locked doors into a maze of corridors.

The door opened onto a lovely restaurant with tables and chairs, even German waitresses who told them the menu. Food was plentiful and eaten with great appetites.

Afterwards they were kitted out with a nursing uniform and blankets, etc. For the time being they were free till morning when they had to be on duty at eight sharp.

Marta went to her room and tried on her uniform. It fitted well but the cap was a problem. She looked at herself in the mirror. 'Hallo, Nurse Kelle!' Now she was tired and sleep offered comfort till morning…

Six o'clock the next morning… Marta didn't waste any time getting ready, except for the hat, but Inge was at hand to make it perfect as they went to the restaurant.

Again the food was good; hot and not rationed. Then it was on to the offices for details of which wards to go to. Now Marta was on her own and quite relieved that no German speaking was allowed on the wards.

Each girl was issued with a key and instructions never to leave a door unlocked at any time. Now Marta was to be judged on her own merit. She entered Ward 14 and a sister greeted her and two Irish nurses took Marta along to the dormitory to start dressing the patients in their bundles of clothes on their beds. She was not too young to handle this and got on with the job. There were forty-five patients. They went to the washrooms and toilets and afterwards settled the patients in their own chairs in a big room. It was all routine work. Soon more staff joined to help with the feeding. Beds had to be made and then later the sister went around with medication and told Marta to assist her; a keen eye for observation was in her favour.

So ended her first day of duty without much trouble, but Marta met the matron on her way out, who spotted her earrings and told her strongly not to forget what kind of patients she was working with. Good advice not to be forgotten. They had to be vigilant at all times. Camp life helped Marta enormously to pass the test. She also befriended two German girls who were married and lived outside the hospital.

The day dawned to test her courage. It was a sunny autumn day. A young nurse on duty with Marta called for assistance to catch a patient, getting coats for them as they were let outside into a high-walled garden.

There was a call of alarm, and the nurse shouted, 'Run over there! Catch her if you can!' Out of the bushes walked a woman, stark naked. She evaded Marta's attempts till another member of staff managed to get a coat over her and she was taken inside again. It never occurred to Marta that they could be dangerous, but it's unwise to tell tales now since the hospital has been demolished.

A new housing estate was all around when Marta returned years later. By coincidence, her own daughter worked from there, passing her diploma from Tone Vale.

Time went by. Marta was keen to learn and she was making progress. Her past was still her past, and was still present at times – the degrading hunger and pain endured.

After a month Marta was called over the intercom to the matron's office. With anxious feelings she located the door.

'Come in.' She stood to attention. The matron smiled. 'Sit down, Marta.' Sister Mary told her the fine standards of work showed in the ward. She could be a good nurse potentially.

Marta's mind was reeling at such a high proposal, but she knew by instinct she was too soft for such a demanding profession.

In all honesty she confessed she was engaged to be married as soon as her time was free. More questions about Stuart. He was actually a trained special orderly in the medical army. Would he come to work here?' Bravely Marta replied she would ask him and she was dismissed, flushed with this new proposal.

That night in her little room of security, she started writing to Stuart, but there was no way for him to leave Blackpool for more reasons than one.

When off duty Marta liked walking around the beautiful

countryside; fresh air was always needed. Germany seemed to fade into the distance. The transition to speaking English came easy. To think, six months had passed in the meantime, not without attention, of course, from the male nurses who shared the dining room, but Marta was no easy catch; she flashed back that she was engaged, end of story.

A Birthday Present

As autumn glory was about in October her birthday was due. 'Nurse Kelle, there is a visitor at the back door,' loud and clear over the intercom. Anxiously she rushed through the now well-known corridors unlocking the doors. A smart Stuart was looking at her. Arm in arm they stood not able to speak. What next? The only solution was to see matron. She was strict but fair. Nervously Marta blurted out it was her Stuart from Blackpool here for her birthday, and to her surprise Matron gave her permission to take him to the restaurant for food, also access to the lounge at the nursing home and if he had no where to stay they should see sister so-and-so who would take him in.

There was also time off for herself. What a birthday present! Proudly she entered the restaurant and sat at a table and the waitress was pleased to help. The other nurses, mostly Irish, made eyes at Marta's precious darling but he only had eyes for Marta, and as they walked outside into the countryside, they noticed a haystack nearby …and lead us not into temptation!

Anyway, they both went into the lounge with everybody else talking about this and that. It was getting late. Marta and Stuart went outside to say goodnight, and whispering they parted. In her room, rolling up a little blanket and with her alarm clock she sneaked out into the night. She found Stuart leaning against a tree, smoking. He touch her excited face, this was not the usual thing to do…

Good show; the hay was dry. As he lifted her up to the top and followed her, they lay under the starlit night, doing what comes naturally to two people in love. Being parted for so long to feel each heart beat close was marvellous, but soon it was time for Marta to part. Tears in her eyes, she kissed him tenderly and slowly then very carefully walked through the wet grass back to the nursing home, hoping that no one would see her; all was well.

Blackpool

SO ENDED ANOTHER REUNION FOR A SHORT TIME. SHE WAS due a holiday planned for Christmas in Blackpool, but Stuart had arranged a transfer to another hospital, so she took her leave and travelled through the night, unaware what trials lay ahead of her.

Early morning in Blackpool: Marta didn't know it was a seaside resort. Her heart started beating as the train came to a halt. People were moving as she scanned for Stuart on the platform, and as she stepped off the train straight into his arms he picked up her case and arm in arm they walked out of the dark station into a magnificent view of the Irish sea – glittering silver in the morning sunlight. Again they were together hand in hand as Stuart guided them through the traffic to a tram stop. They looked at each other intensely while waiting for a tram. Lovingly he helped her up the steps. It was so new to her, looking at all the hotels on the promenade.

Bispham – here they got off. Ahead was Cavendish Road and Marta put her arm through his to feel secure. Suddenly he pointed to a woman on the other side. 'There's Mam, let's go over,' and then he introduced her to his mother. Instinctively Marta didn't feel at ease, looking at the grim face that said it all – *You're taking my son from me...*

Shaking she clutched his arm to her body. 'She will love you,' he assured her. Walking along past some nice houses, at number 95 they stopped, and through a gate entered the house. A little lady stood there to greet Marta. At least she was smiling!

'This is Miss Hopkinson, our landlady,' Stuart said.

Miss Hopkinson kindly replied, 'Pleased to meet you.'

What a relief to find someone friendly!

Marta followed Stuart into a room. Closing the door sharply he took her into his arms. At last! He pressed her close. They kissed, just to make it seem real; together forever, heaven on earth.

Stuart went to the scullery to make a cup of tea while Marta looked around the room. It was not very big with old furniture, but she noticed a piano. 'A nice hot cup of tea, my darling,' he announced, sitting down at the table.

As Mam reappeared, she seemed a very Victorian lady who hardly ever smiled. As she asked what to make for super, Stuart had to try to guide her mood into warmer waters. A nice meal was provided in no time, and Stuart talked mostly, trying his best. Marta sensed this was a difficult situation to handle, and didn't know what to expect of her.

Later Stuart explained to her that his father had left her for another woman and taken all the money and savings; no wonder she was bitter!

Anyhow, by now Marta was getting tired from her journey, so the arrangement was for her to sleep in the big bedroom while Mam slept in a small room and Stuart had to sleep downstairs on the settee so there was no hanky-panky. Marta went upstairs after saying goodnight and went into the allocated bedroom. She noticed it was furnished with a mahogany bedroom suite – very nice, like home in a way. She slipped into the double bed. Oh my God! It was so cold! But never mind; she was tired enough and went to sleep. The bathroom and toilet were on the next landing.

Mam greeted Marta in a solemn way, but little Miss Hopkinson was of a more cheerful disposition that made her more at ease.

Wedding Bells

THE DAY WAS SPENT GETTING TO KNOW MORE ABOUT everything. As Mam was out working Stuart suggested they go to the hospital about a job. Stuart announced all was well – the hospital accepted her for work, but first Marta had to go to the Labour Exchange. So as Stuart had to go to work he showed her the way to find it. She entered the place and was in for a shock. The assistant was telling her off for leaving Tone Vale without permission. She was a German under contract; they decided when she could move elsewhere.

The message was to return to Tone Vale. The words were hitting hard and the bottom fell from under her feet. The assistant noted Marta was upset. 'Okay,' she said, 'you have still holiday time left, but nothing can change the situation.'

Shaken, Marta crossed the street to catch a tram for Cavendish Road, thinking deeply about what was said and how being a German she was trained to obey the law not to be led astray. She felt guilty and hurt because Marta was a very serious woman, not so young as Stuart, but with principles of her own.

When he arrived for his lunch, Mam told him she was crying upstairs.

Immediately he rushed to her side and assured her they would sort it all out.

'We'll find a way out, we'll go together this afternoon, I promise,' and so he did.

Stuart was now in charge. 'What can stop her from having to go back? We are getting married in June!' That was news to Marta! But the assistant replied, 'No change.'

Unless they got married straightaway she'd have to go.

'All right, we will just do that,' and with that remark they both left and headed home; Marta was still not convinced as to what was going on. Sitting on the bed, tears still falling down her cheeks, she saw Stuart on his knee proposing marriage to her. She loved him as much as he did her and so nodded in the affirmative. He went downstairs to tell his mother of his decision. Now she was crying. It was all so sudden. He had to have her consent not being twenty-one till May.

Afterwards as Marta's holiday was running short, action had to be taken. All the documents were gathered and they went to see the magistrate.

'Come on now, cheer up,' Stuart teased her. 'Getting married can't be bad, let's have a cup of tea and then we'll go and sort it all out.' He was a tower of strength, so positive. She had never experienced such support before. He cared and he wanted her. *Strong feelings in such a young chap*. She herself was afraid such powerful love could go wrong, but he'd already told her in Hamburg he would return.

Miss Hopkinson was delighted about a wedding, beaming with pleasure at the prospect. Mam couldn't help noticing this and tried to be more cheerful herself. The next thing was to get some nice outfits for Marta. Stuart took her to a shop – he knew the girl working there and he introduced her. 'This is Elsie. She will see you right.' He also invited Elsie to be a bridesmaid and her boyfriend to be his best man.

So the time was all set for the wedding date; it was raining and dark outside. Stuart sat at the piano playing the Third Man tune. The waited for the taxi and then every action went smoothly and was well organised, as Stuart and Marta were pronounced man and wife. There was a meal afterwards and then to the pictures. No blessing, not in white, no organ playing, but nevertheless Stuart was Marta's Mr Right. His love projected an energy into her to make him proud of her. This marriage was built on true love. 'Until death do us part…'

Printed in the United Kingdom
by Lightning Source UK Ltd.
101253UKS00001B/184-255